CRITICAL PRAISE FOR *THE SOLOMON SISTERS WISE UP*

"Senate scored high with *See Jane Date* (2001), and she now presents another winner that will have readers cheering for the warm, witty, and lovable Solomon sisters as they wise up, find romance, and learn to love each other."
—*Booklist*

"An empowering and witty tale of three sisters who learn it's OK to be exactly who they are.... Readers will find themselves caring about what happens to each of these three very different sisters."
—*Romantic Times*

CRITICAL PRAISE FOR *SEE JANE DATE*

"*See Jane Date* tells the tale of a smart, funny 28-year-old editor at a Manhattan publishing house who has been trapped in a 2-year date drought. Alas, she must dig up a presentable boyfriend to accompany her to her cousin's fancy wedding. The mad date dash is on."
—*USA TODAY*

"...a refreshing change of pace..."
—*Publishers Weekly*

"Senate's prose is fresh and lively."
—*Boston Globe*

"It's fun to watch Jane bumble her way through the singles scene and find out that sometimes people aren't what they first appear. Senate's debut is both witty and snappy."
—*Booklist*

"The story unfolds like a brightly wrapped bonbon. It's tantalizing and tasty..."
—*Sacramento Bee*

melissa senate

whose wedding is it anyway?

RED
DRESS
INK
™

First edition December 2004

WHOSE WEDDING IS IT ANYWAY?

A Red Dress Ink novel

ISBN 0-373-25077-0

www.RedDressInk.com

Printed in U.S.A.

To Karen Hirsch and Lucia Macro,
two very cool women.

ACKNOWLEDGMENTS

Endless thanks to my editor, the one and only
Joan Marlow Golan, for her editorial brilliance and
constant encouragement.

Enormous thanks to Margaret Marbury, executive editor
of Red Dress Ink, and to the entire RDI team, with
extraspecial xoxo to the very talented Margie Miller
for the covers.

Gleeful thanks to my agent, the amazing Kim Witherspoon.

I grew up at Harlequin from 1988 to 1998 and owe more
than I can say to Isabel Swift, Tara Hughes Gavin,
Leslie Wainger, Leslie Kazanjian, Lucia Macro,
Karen Taylor Richman and Tracy Boggier.

Kissy-poo thanks to Sarah Mlynowski for her generosity
(and hilarious novels).

There aren't enough thanks in the world for Diane Trummer,
baby-sitter extraordinaire.

*Muchas gracias a Jennifer Verenzuela maravillosa y su
madre, Nancy.*

Thanks to Sharon Erickson Horton, for the adorable
drumsticks joke and to the Yahoo Chick Litters for always
being there.

TIA to the New York UrbanBaby Toddler Parents message
board moms, for making procrastination from writing so
informative and fun.

Loving thanks to my mother, sister and brother for their
support.

Happy thanks to the Kemplers, Marcia and Peter,
Matthew and Kit, for the warm family welcome and the
"We'll baby-sit Max. Go take a few hours for yourself."

To my precious Max, for existing.

And to Adam, for everything.

chapter 1

If there were a Top Ten list for Most Embarrassing Bridesmaid Dress, say on *Late Show with David Letterman,* the two hanging in the back of my closet would take spots. It wasn't that my two closest friends (one engaged, one married) had bad taste. It was that they had handed over control of their weddings to bossy relatives.

For example, let's say that your best friend Jane's aunt Ina was paying for her July Fourth wedding and insisted on an Independence Day theme (yet failed to see the irony in that). You might find yourself spending two hundred and sixty bucks on a red, white and blue striped dress with stars on the straps. The bridesmaid dress equivalent of the American flag.

"I could either live a good life, a *sane* life for the next six months," Jane had said in self-defense, "or I could spend the next six months arguing with Aunt Ina, who reminds me every day that *she's* paying for my wedding. I choose my sanity."

And so Jane spent her weekend afternoons pricing tri-dyed (guess which colors?) peau de soie shoes with a two-inch kitten heel.

Embarrassing dress number two was an iridescent purple taffeta, the stiffest ever made. It was your standard-issue hideous bridesmaid dress, with tiny polka-dot bows along the neckline and a huge polka-dot bow on the butt. Amanda's very intimidating mother-in-law had paid for her huge Southern wedding—enough said there.

Despite the flag dress and the polka-dot bows, Jane and Amanda were now staring at the bridesmaid dress they would wear at *my* wedding as though it were worse.

Okay, it was.

Much, much worse.

My bridal party, a co-worker's bridal party and half the staff of *Wow Weddings* magazine were squeezed inside It's Your Day bridal salon, staring at a mannequin wearing...*was* that a dress, actually?

"This dress would be perfect for your bridesmaids, Eloise!" raved Astrid O'Connor, editor in chief of *Wow Weddings*. She stood next to the mannequin she had moments ago unveiled with the flourish and megawatt smile of a game-show hostess.

Uh, isn't there a door number two?

"This is payback, right?" Jane and Amanda whispered to me in unison.

"No payback," I whispered back. "That's the point."

No paying at all. Not one penny. This shopping trip at It's Your Day was my first foray into the "free dream wedding" I'd been promised in exchange for being featured as Today's Modern Bride in *Wow Weddings*. I, Eloise Manfred, was going to plan my wedding, every single iota of it, in the pages of *Wow Weddings*. I'd be photographed choosing my wedding gown, the shoes, the flowers, the caterer, the reception site, the invitations—the everything. Tens of thousands of *Wow* readers would see me checking out the posh Hudson Hotel and the Waldorf-Astoria for reception sites. I'd be photographed at Tiffany's on Fifth Avenue, snootily rejecting ten-thousand-dollar wedding bands that just weren't The One.

All expenses paid! All *I* had to do was point at what I wanted and smile for the camera for my picture spread in America's least favorite bridal magazine. *Wow* was no *Modern Bride.* The not-so-famous Astrid O'Connor had been promoted or demoted, depending on how you looked at it, from the much better performing *Wow Woman* magazine, to turn *Wow Weddings*'s numbers around (circulation was at an all-time low). One of her brilliant ideas to increase advertising revenue was to feature two real-life engaged women as Today's Modern Bride and Today's Classic Bride, who would wear, eat and register for whatever the advertisers wanted to feature and sell millions of. That little nugget of information would be kept from the readers, of course.

Look, readers—our Modern Bride, Eloise Manfred, has "chosen" Overpriced-and-Not-Worth-It Brand's Wedding Gown, Same As Any Other Photographer and Super Rubber Chicken Caterers for her dream wedding—and so should you, brides-to-be-of-America!

According to Astrid, I would become a major trendsetter, like Sarah Jessica Parker and the Hilton sisters.

But if the bridesmaid dress that Astrid had chosen for me was an indication of what was in store for modern brides of America, I could pretty much count on making Blackwell's Worst-Dressed List. I could forget about Tiffany's too.

Talk about handing over control. I was beginning to have the sneaking suspicion that I'd sold my soul to the wedding devil.

Four days ago, the free dream wedding had seemed like an unturndownable offer. Astrid had overheard me and Philippa Wills, recently engaged departmental editorial assistant, oohing and aahing over my diamond ring in *Wow*'s tiny kitchenette. Astrid (who I'd dubbed Acid after my last performance review) ordered us both inside her office. I'd expected to get the *Eloise, as you're still quite green at magazines, you should spend your spare moments learning the business instead of chatting* routine. I'd been working at *Wow* for almost two years, but was still considered "quite green" because the bulk of my work experience had been designing book covers for a publishing house and not glossy magazine layouts.

As Philippa quaked next to me, I waited for the "Here At *Wow*" speech, but instead, Astrid ordered the intern to bring in coffee for three, then explained to Philippa and me that our engagement rings had given her a major brainstorm. The sight of Philippa and me standing next to each other (a rare occurrence) had apparently stopped her in her tracks. There was Philippa, with her sleek white-blond hair, pale green shirtwaist dress (Ralph Lauren, of course) and Ferragamo penny loafers. And there was I, with the "*crazily* cut auburn hair" (I wouldn't say crazily), weird shoes and Le Chateau ensemble. According to Astrid, Philippa and I represented two opposite ends of the bridal spectrum: the Classic Bride and her traditional taste (Philippa) versus the Modern Bride and her edgy taste (that would be me).

If we would allow *Wow Weddings* to feature us as real-life bride-to-be models in the June issue as we made our wedding plans and "chose" our gowns and caterers and invitations and kept cute wedding-plans diaries detailing our every hot pick, *Wow* and its advertisers would pay for our weddings, which she estimated at a hundred thousand dollars apiece—"to do it right, of course."

"Of course," Philippa and I had repeated in shocked unison.

"You do understand that we'll have to hustle," Astrid said. "We're almost ready to put the May issue to bed. That means we'll only have about six weeks to plan your entire weddings."

Fine with us! We shouted our yeses like shampooees in a Clairol Herbal Essences commercial. Two hours later, we signed long contracts that we didn't bother reading. Hey, we had whirlwind weddings to plan!

When I told Noah about the deal I'd made with Astrid, he kissed me on the lips and said, "Whatever makes you happy is fine with me." Then he added, "But you do know there's no such thing as a free wedding, right?"

"Eloise, shall the fashion editor document this dress as your selection for bridesmaid dress?" asked Astrid with a snap of impatience.

Amanda leaned close and whispered, "You're not really going to make us wear that, are you? It's the ugliest thing I've ever seen!"

Amanda wasn't prone to exaggeration. I hadn't seen every woman's collection of embarrassing bridesmaid dresses, but I could safely say that number one on the Letterman Top Ten list would go to the metallic, coffee-col-

ored, asymmetrical rubber oddity complete with collar
that Astrid was pushing on me.

"The hue! The fabrication! The lines!" Astrid gushed.

The absolute hideousness was more like it.

Everyone was staring at me. My bridal party—which
consisted of Jane Gregg, Amanda Frank Jorgensen, Natasha Nutley (yes, *that* Natasha Nutley), Beth Benjamin (my
fiancé's sister) and Philippa Wills—were all surreptitiously
shaking their heads. (Please note that I didn't have a maid
of honor as Astrid had deemed that role too traditional.)
Philippa's bridal party (three white-blond, preppy, head-
banded women who looked remarkably like Philippa and
yet were her fiancé's sisters) were staring from me to the
dress. And the staff of *Wow Weddings* was waiting with half
dread, half glee for me to dare tell Astrid O'Connor no.
That I most certainly would not force my bridesmaids, my
dearest friends (well, three of them anyway), to wear that
so-called dress.

"Eloise," Astrid said, beaming at the bridesmaid dress
from outer space, "it's my experienced opinion that this
particular dress's edgy aura is the manifestation of modern and reflects the tastes of today's Modern Bride."

"More like Star Trek bride," Natasha whispered in my
ear.

"Star Trek *Next* Generation," I whispered back.

"Eloise, we're waiting," Astrid droned. "Your choice,
please. If you prefer a dress other than the one I feel is best
suited to your party, you may choose from this rack or that
rack only." Her beige talons pointed at two racks with my
name on them. Across the aisle were two racks with Philippa's name. Everything else in the store was off limits.

There is no such thing as a free wedding....

Astrid O'Connor's vision of modern was quite different from mine. From most anyone's on earth, I imagined. A problem, given that next week we were choosing wedding gowns, and my dream dress, on display in It's Your Day's window, was as far from edgy as you could get. Simple white satin and very feminine, the gown was timeless, elegant. My plan was to use Astrid's own fashion doublespeak to convince her that the gown's very unedginess made it edgy.

"Eloise, *shall* we go with this atmosphere-colored dress for your bridesmaids?" Astrid asked, her trademark dark red lips forming into a tight smile.

Atmosphere? Try *unflushed toilet bowl.* "Astrid, it's very interesting from a fashion-forward standpoint, but I really have my heart set on *that* dress for my bridesmaids." I pointed at a floaty pink satin dress in the "forbidden" area, its only aura Audrey Hepburn.

Until I saw the *A Midsummer Night's Dream* dress on a rack off limits to me, I didn't even know I cared about bridesmaids' dresses. Or headpieces, veils or dyed-to-match peau de soie shoes.

I didn't even know—for absolute certain—that I wanted to marry Noah Benjamin.

I take that back. I take that back. I take that back.

Cold feet. It was just a case of cold feet.

You are engaged to be married. You said yes. You love Noah. You've loved Noah for the past two years. From the moment you met him. You've been waiting for him to propose since your third date.

You're getting married in the pages of a national magazine, for God's sake.

"You're not *one hundred* percent sure you want to marry Noah and you've signed on the dotted line to appear as a real-life bride in a wedding magazine?" asked Amanda, ever the practical paralegal, when I'd piped up with my ambivalence a few days ago. "What if you break the engagement—you could get fired!"

"I think that's why Eloise agreed to be featured," Jane had put in. "So she *couldn't* weasel out of the engagement."

I had weaseled out of an engagement once before. The wrong engagement. Everyone in my life agreed with me on that. This one, this five-day-old engagement to Noah Benjamin, very good-looking, very sweet, very smart, immensely lovable Noah Benjamin, was the right engagement.

Astrid was staring at me. "Eloise, you may choose only from *this* rack or *that* rack."

This rack or that rack were filled with one outer-space dress after another. I slid monstrosity after monstrosity along the racks, praying that one would be tolerable. I settled for not-asymmetrical.

"I'll go with this," I said, holding up a shiny dark purple minidress that felt like one of those thin, rubbery Halloween masks of a monster or ex-president.

Price tag: $2,300.

I glanced at my bridesmaids. Jane, Amanda and Natasha (all of whom I *asked* to be my bridesmaids, and Beth and Philippa (both of whom *told* me they were going to be my bridesmaids) had variations of relief and "But that one isn't much better!" on their faces.

Astrid was disappointed. "Eloise, it's my experienced opinion that this one—" she held up the toilet-bowl dress "—would suit your bridal party better."

Yeah, because rubber felt great against the skin. And because the color of dog poop—metallic dog poop, at that—looked fabulous with every skin tone. And who didn't love a collar on a formal dress!

All heads whipped to me.

"But, Astrid, you did say this rack or that rack," I responded. "And I did find this on *that* rack."

She peered at me over the top of her silly square eyeglasses, then swiveled on her high heels. Her pristine white cashmere wrap almost hit me in the face. "Ellen, document Eloise's selection," she instructed the fashion editor.

Ah, victory. Pyrrhic, but it still felt good.

Astrid turned to the articles editor, Maura, whom everyone secretly called "Mini-Astrid." With her copycat Louise Brooks bob, tiny eyeglasses and fake pashmina wrap, Maura looked exactly like Astrid, except that Astrid was five-ten and Maura five-two. "Maura, for the bridesmaid-dress sidebar, highlight the many Post-Mod brand dresses at It's Your Day and how Eloise loved them all so much that she spent the night on a lovely lace-covered cot in a large private dressing room in the tony bridal salon 'to sleep' on her selection. She awoke from a dream about the raven-eggplant dress sans neck accompaniment and knew it was the one for her bridal party. Note that she called her bridesmaids, who rushed over at the crack of dawn to see her selection. Discuss in detail the colors, fabrics and price points, which celebrities the dresses would suit, such as the Hilton sisters, Sarah Jessica, Britney, Christina and Pink, and add that Natalie Portman and Hilary Duff were rumored to have been spotted trying on Post-Mod brand dresses. Find out if we can get at least a B-list actress who recently married to agree to 'look' at the dress."

Mini-Astrid was writing in her tiny notebook so fast she was risking carpal tunnel syndrome. As Astrid droned on, amid choruses of "That's brilliant, Astrid!" from the more butt-kissing of her minions, the non-*Wow* contingent's eyes popped open with *Is she kidding?* astonishment. She wasn't.

Astrid clapped. "All right, Modern Bridesmaids. Please begin taking your places around the Modern Bride, gazing at her and the dress."

Wow Weddings's photographer, the award-winning Devlin of the first name only, clicked shut his cell phone and popped off his chair, a huge camera around his neck. He might have been good-looking if he weren't such a complete jerk. He snapped, literally, at his assistant, a pretty twenty-something with a crew cut, who quickly set up the lighting.

Devlin arranged us around a mannequin now wearing the shiny purple dress. "You with the dark hair," he said, gesturing at Jane. "Your shirt is all wrong—the color is awful on you and boatnecks are for twelve-year-olds." He snapped again at his assistant, and she tossed a long, double-breasted black leather coat at Jane, who raised an eyebrow but put it on. "You with the streaks of gray—" he upped his chin at Beth "—If you could rinse with some Nice 'n Easy before the next shoot and tweeze your eyebrows, that would be great." He turned his attention to Amanda. "Blondie, you're going to have to stand sideways with an arm across your chest as you reach to touch the dress—that way, your breasts won't take the focus off the shot and detract from the bride."

This was very likely the first time a man called for Amanda's breasts to be downplayed.

This was also Devlin in a good mood. Luckily, Jane and Amanda seemed to find him an object of great fun, a caricature of a caricature. The more insulting he was, the more they had to restrain themselves from bursting into laughter. And Noah's sister, whom I barely knew, was too busy hating her soon-to-be ex-husband to even notice another jerk.

Devlin shook his head at Philippa. "Philippa, we'll need to tone down your prettiness for Eloise's bridal-party shots. Let's put your hair in two heroin-chic braids—" He snapped, and his assistant jumped up and whipped Philippa's long, straight white-blond hair into elastic bands. "Much better. Wipe off her girlie lipstick and add some brown-red gloss."

"I look awfully washed out without my pink lipstick," Philippa squeaked.

"That's the point," Devlin said as Philippa was transformed into East Village chic. "All right, people—gaze adoringly at Eloise and delight in the dress."

"What about her?" Philippa asked, pointing at Natasha.

Devlin glanced at Natasha Nutley, taking in her Nicole Kidman ringlets, her gorgeous green eyes, her height, her skinniness, her Anthropologie outfit. "*She* is absolutely perfect as is."

Jane and I shared a knowing smile. Two years ago, Natasha had been Jane's archenemy, mainly for being as perfect as Devlin affirmed. Now, Jane's former nemesis was one of our best friends. Even Natasha's two-year-old daughter was perfect. At the moment, baby Summer was clapping in the corner as an It's Your Day staffer waved an Elmo puppet at her.

Devlin snapped his camera and mouth for a half hour. Jane, Amanda, Natasha, Beth and Philippa could barely smile near the end.

Astrid clapped twice for attention. "Modern Bridesmaids, please move to the dressing rooms to be fitted. Philippa, we already have your measurements, so stay put."

The other four women trailed after the fashion editor.

As they disappeared into the dressing rooms, Jane, Amanda and Natasha shook their heads in wonder.

"You don't get sanity *or* the wedding you want?" Jane had asked when I told her about the deal I'd made with Astrid.

Okay, I got neither. The key word for me (at the time, anyway) had been *free*. I didn't have an aunt who'd been putting away money for my wedding for years. I didn't have a mother-in-law with an antebellum mansion in Louisiana to spare for my wedding. What I did have was a mother-in-law-to-be who announced at least twice a conversation that she and her husband considered themselves "traditionalists."

The day after Noah and I got engaged, Noah's parents and sister had come over to celebrate our engagement with deli sandwiches and a family-size bag of potato chips. "What I mean by traditionalist, dear," his mother explained, "is that *traditionally*, the *bride's* parents pay for the wedding."

Noah coughed and reminded his parents that it was just me and my postman's widow grandmother and had been for a long time, and Mrs. Benjamin coughed back too and said that young people today were very resourceful and that they'd be happy to contribute a lovely deli platter for twenty-five people if we wanted to marry in their living room. Oh, and she'd even move their coffee table to accommodate one or two additional folding chairs.

"Well, I really appreciate that, Mrs. Benjamin," I'd said. "But I have my heart set on a traditional wedding. You know—the works."

"The works are very expensive, dear," she responded.

I had two hundred and seventy dollars in my bank account. Noah had fourteen hundred.

"There's always Vegas," he told me.

I shook my head.

"There's always our living room," Mrs. Benjamin sing-songed. "You could choose your color scheme to match—green with gold accents. Beth looks fabulous in green. As one of your bridesmaids, she should have input into the dress, by the way."

As one of my bridesmaids? I'd had three conversations with Beth Benjamin, all lasting twenty to forty seconds, all about the weather. Did you automatically ask your fiancé's sister to be in your wedding party?

"I look best in a jewel-toned green, not muted or mossy," Beth contributed.

Mrs. Benjamin nodded. "In fact, Eloise, your gown should have a greenish cast, an ivory with a slight greenish tint, so that the colors blend. You're not going to wear white-white, are you? I mean, you and Noah have been *living together* for the past two months."

That night, I'd dreamed (nightmared) that I was walking down the aisle in a mossy-green wedding gown to Noah, whose head had been replaced by a quarter pound of liverwurst. I'd burst into tears, waking Noah, who pulled me into his arms and told me we'd figure something out, that everything would be okay, and I thought, *Yes, yes, yes—everything will be okay, I can marry you, after all. You are the one for me. Of course I meant yes.* The next morning, when Astrid offered me the free hundred-thousand-dollar wedding, I couldn't say yes fast enough.

chapter 2

"On to the Classic Bride," Astrid announced with yet another clap of her hands. "Philippa, make your choice from your two racks. You have five minutes."

Poor Philippa. At least I'd had *ten* minutes. Such was the perk of being an associate staffer instead of an assistant.

Two years ago, after getting downsized from Posh Publishing and suffering through an exhausting job search, I'd been hired by Astrid on a probationary basis as associate art associate. "You were promoted to assistant art director only a few months before you were 'let go' at Posh, so you didn't have time to learn the job," she'd said. "Here at *Wow,* we have to *do* the job before we can *fulfill* the promise of the title." If I hadn't been so desperate, I would have gone back to calling every contact I'd ever made and circling ads in the *Times.* I accepted the position at *Wow Weddings* magazine with the rationalization that my prepromotion title at Posh had been *assistant* art associate, so, in a way, *Wow* was a step up.

Philippa zoomed for her own forbidden zone, to a rack on the outskirts of my Modern area. "I am *so* in love with this one! Isn't it just fabulous?"

Superfabulous was more like it. A strange muted yellow and sparkly, with a low-cut halter-style top, mermaid-cut skirt covered with yellow feathers and a huge Sarah Jessica Parker/Carrie Bradshaw feather-flower on the left breast, the gown hardly seemed preppy Philippa Wills's style— or the least bit classic.

"Yes, yes, yes! This is definitely my choice for my wedding gown," Philippa said, holding it up against her tall, willowy frame in the floor-length mirror on the wall. "With the right makeup, I'll look fabu in yellow!"

You'll look like Big Bird, was my first thought. Not that Philippa would wear the dress; Astrid would nix it in two seconds.

"No. Absolutely not," Astrid came in on cue with one shake of her head. Her poker-straight platinum bob didn't move. "Does that look like a *traditional* gown to you, Philippa? As our *Classic* Bride, you must choose a *traditional* gown. In any case, we're not choosing wedding gowns today."

Philippa pouted and fingered the flower on the Big Bird dress. "But it's my *dream* gown. I love it. I don't see why yellow can't be considered trad—"

"You may choose your bridal party's dresses from *this* rack—" Astrid swiveled to extend an entire arm at a rack of your standard-fare-bridesmaid dress in every color "—or *that* rack."

My bridesmaids poked their heads out of the dressing rooms. While Astrid was busy glaring at Philippa, Jane was mouthing *this rack or that rack* while Amanda and Natasha were pointing exaggeratedly to the left and right.

Beth, sister-in-law-to-be, stared back and forth from Philippa to Astrid. As an accountant in a tax-law firm, Beth didn't ordinarily come in contact with pouters or Dragon Ladies with tiny square eyeglasses and cashmere wraps the size of a bed.

"Philippa, I have a meeting at five-thirty," Astrid said. "You have two minutes left to make your choice before I make it for you."

Philippa glanced from the boring rack on the left to the more boring one on the right, then slid each dress along the rack as tears pooled in her eyes.

"This one's gorgeous, Philippa," I said, spying the floaty pink *Midsummer's Night Dream* dress buried in the middle of her "this" rack. "It's very 'I'd Like To Thank the Academy,' like you said you wanted."

She glanced at the dress and her face lit up. She was relatively easy to please, if you knew how to do it. "Oooh, yes! It's lovely! Good eye, Eloise. We'll all look good in pink." She glanced at her fiancé's sisters; they bobbed their heads and smiled. Philippa beamed. "Okay, I made my choice."

"Fine," Astrid said. "Fashion editor, please speak with It's Your Day's manager about ordering the maid of honor's version—it will be almost the same, but with special beading detail on the empire waist." She glanced up. "Which one of you is the maid of honor?"

The three blondes glanced at me. I glanced at them. None of us said, *I am!*

"Um, actually, I haven't chosen my maid of honor yet," Philippa said. "I have *so* many girlfriends and it's *so* hard to choose! But my top three choices for the honor of standing up for me are all a size four."

Oh brother.

"Places, people!" Astrid barked with a clap of her hands.

Devlin began arranging Philippa's bridesmaids, her fiancé's three sisters and me. As the sisters were all queens of classic, he had very little to do insultwise other than making me borrow a peach cardigan sweater and insisting I remove my tiny green pterodactyl earrings. We gazed, we smiled, we fake oohed and aahed.

This was actually our second day of fake oohing and fake aahing for the camera. Yesterday Philippa and I had taken some preliminary "I'm So Happy I'm a Bride-to-Be" shots in front of the very classic Tavern on the Green in Central Park and the very modern Puck Building in SoHo.

Devlin had ordered me to look happier, to glow more. Difficult to do when you suddenly weren't so sure your fiancé was really Mr. Right.

"Like this," Philippa had said to me, and strangely enough, on cue, her face lit up.

Then and now, as she glowed for each snap of Devlin's camera, I realized I was jealous of her. Jealous that she was so sure of her future, her fiancé.

I was desperate for a girls' night out, but Jane, Amanda and Natasha all had after-the-dress-selection plans. Jane and Amanda were heading to a *pre*-prenatal yoga class (I kid you not) "for those just thinking about womb flexibility," and Natasha had a playdate in a sandbox. Even Noah, who was pretty good at girl talk, had plans tonight.

"Okay, it's a wrap," Astrid announced with a jangle of the five thick silver bangles on her emaciated wrist. "As it's four-fifteen, I've decided not to require you to return to the office."

What a gal!

"Philippa and Eloise," Astrid continued, "your diary entries about this shopping trip are due first thing Monday morning. I want two hundred and fifty words, perky, lots of exclamation points." She flipped through pages on her clipboard. "Which one of you has the deceased mother? I can't find it in my notes."

You could hear the clichéd pin drop. The *Wow* staffers darted uncomfortable glances at me and Philippa.

What a complete shithead Astrid was. I glanced at Jane, whose mother had also passed away. Jane raised an eyebrow, but didn't hurl a rubber dress at Astrid.

"That would be me," I said, my cheeks burning.

"El-o-ise," Astrid said in slow motion as she jotted down *Dead Mother: Eloise.* "Your diary entry should focus on the poignancy of shopping for your bridal party without Mother. It's a strong human-interest point for our readership." She thought for a moment. "Yes, a theme of Mother's unfulfilled dream—to see her little girl married."

My mother's dream for me *was* to marry. But for much more complicated reasons than Astrid's backward baloney.

Before I could even formulate an evil thought about Astrid, she moved on. "I'm going to have your final wedding-plans schedules for you on Monday," she continued, "but don't plan *anything*—a manicure, drinks with friends, even a headache—for the next eight weeks until you receive your schedule. Also, family-photo shoots will take place one month from now. That way, family members who need to fly in can make arrangements. You'll receive the exact dates in your schedule packet."

Oh God. Oh God. Oh God.

"Um, Astrid, what if my father or brother can't come

to the shoots?" I asked around the lump in my throat. "Just in case, I mean."

"Simple," she responded. "You hire stand-ins. You contact one of the model agencies we use or even an escort service and inform them you're looking for a fatherly type and a brother type with your coloring. In fact, stand-ins are even better than the real thing, since they're invariably more attractive, and readers like attractive real-life models. If you do need to hire stand-ins, make sure they have an urban appeal as befits relatives of the Modern Bride. If your real family *is* able to come, we'll enhance their 'hip and cool factor' for the shoots. Same goes for you, Philippa, but with a Classic enhancement."

My brother would please Astrid. Twenty-nine-year-old Emmett Manfred was as hip and cool as you got. But he was also who-knew-where, probably thinking deeply on a hill in Oregon or sleeping with a few rich, older women on Park Avenue for rent money. I hadn't seen or spoken to my brother in over a year.

As for my father, I had no idea if he was hip and cool. Actually, I'd bet my life savings that he was the furthest thing from cool there could possibly be. I hadn't seen or heard from Theo Manfred since I was five years old.

"Thank you all for coming, bridesmaids," Astrid said. She flipped her wrap over her shoulder, snapped on her Jackie O. sunglasses and left It's Your Day, disappearing into a black sedan double-parked in front.

Noah's sister eyed me, said, "We'll discuss later," and huffed out.

Philippa and her future sisters-in-law, chattering excitedly, followed.

Jane, Amanda and Natasha took one last look at the rubber bridesmaid dress.

"The dress isn't half as bad as your boss!" Amanda said, pulling a Fair Isle hat over her shiny blond head.

"It's not a quarter as bad," Natasha put in. "What a witch."

Jane nodded. "Hey, maybe you could hire a stand-in for Astrid. A boss with normal, decent, human appeal!"

They laughed, then all peered at me.

"Are you okay?" Jane asked, her best-friend brown eyes searching mine.

I nodded. "It's just a dress."

"That wasn't what I meant," she whispered.

"I'm okay." Sort of. Not really.

"Amanda, what do you say we skip pre-prenatal yoga and help Summer make Elmo sand pies instead?" Jane asked.

Amanda nodded. "Sounds good to me."

Natasha settled Summer into her stroller and clicked her harness into place. "Summer will be thrilled to have her honorary aunts at her playdate. Eloise, you can come, can't you?"

"Sure," I said.

Did I mention how grateful I was for my friends?

"Elmo! Elmo!" Summer shouted.

Jane squeezed my hand. "El, if it's any consolation, the dress you're wearing in my wedding is worse."

"No, I think they're tied," Amanda said.

Jane laughed and slung an arm around my shoulder. "C'mon, my girl. To the sandbox for a much-needed session of the Flirt Night Round Table."

Twenty-two-month-old Summer Nutley was the most recent member of the Flirt Night Round Table, so named for the flirting the adult members used to do pre-serious relationships and the intimate discussions on every topic imaginable: love, work, sex, men, money, family and life in general. The Flirt Night Round Table began on a street corner eight years ago, when Jane and Amanda and I worked in the same building and became friends over puffs of cigarettes (none of us smoke anymore).

Natasha Nutley might have been a glam celebrity (she'd written a bestselling memoir about her love affair with a famous actor and had a small role on *All My Children* as a nurse), but soon after she became a weekly member of the Flirt Night Round Table two years ago, our group's name could easily have been changed to the *Frump* Night Round Table. The Frump *Afternoon* Round Table (we rarely met at night anymore, unless Natasha could get a baby-sitter). Two years ago, Jane had gotten hot and heavy with boyfriend-now-fiancé Ethan Miles, Amanda had gotten engaged to now-husband Jeff Jorgensen, Natasha had been pregnant and recuperating from way too much heartache and I'd given up flirting and nicotine for long walks and then met Noah.

Flirting, dating, sex—all the juicy talk had been replaced by relationship talk. Wedding talk. Baby talk. I knew just about every detail of Ethan's and Jeff's and baby Summer's lives. Ethan's favorite food. Jeff's least favorite sexual position. Summer's frequency of bowel movements. What Ethan's childhood had been. How long Jeff's penis was. The size of Summer's skull. How Ethan liked his eggs. And my friends knew that Noah was amazing in bed. But had the World's Most Annoying Mother. And whispered "I love you" in my ear every night before he drifted off to sleep. And, because I'd changed Summer's diaper at least a hundred times during baby-sitting duty, I even knew the color and consistency of her poop. If I weren't a diaper changer, I'd know anyway from our Frump Afternoon Round Tables.

Did it sound boring? It wasn't. The new focus of the Flirt Night Round Table was everything we didn't even know we wanted, baby poop included. Until I met Noah, I'd been a serial dater. I'd been famous for meeting guys everywhere—ATM machines, bars, the frozen-food aisle of supermarkets, newspaper kiosks, work, blind dates (Amanda's hubby had way too many available-for-a-reason friends, which Jane could attest to, pre-Ethan), red lights, vending machines, museums. Once, I'd even met a guy while sunbathing on my fire escape. He was on his fire escape, across the street, and he held up a giant sketch pad that said: *Got Suntan Lotion?* We dated for a month before he ditched me for a woman with a summer share in the Hamptons.

I'd also been famous for dating all kinds of men, nationalities, colors, sizes, shapes, personalities. There'd been interesting so-so-looking guys. Dull hunks. Raging activists. I'd been to every kind of religious dinner with various relatives. Seders. Greek Orthodox Easter dinners. Kwanza celebrations.

I hadn't always been a serial dater. There was Lee in high school, the love of my young life and the breakup of all breakups until Michael in college, who had surpassed Lee as both the love of my young life and the breakup of all breakups. And then there was the dating. A lot of dating. Two and a half years ago there was the mini-engagement for three weeks with Serge, a very sweet guy I'd dated for four months. But between college at twenty-one and Noah at thirty-two, I'd been the dating queen of the eastern seaboard. After a thousand dates and a thousand stories to tell my friends over brunch or at Flirt Night Round Table get-togethers, I started itching for something else, something more.

Something truly fun, like love.

And then I met Noah. Noah, with his silky dark hair, hazel-green eyes, dimple in left cheek, and collection of ties with tiny cartoon animals. It was Snoopy when I met him. And little Lucys. Snoopy, spinning around doing the Snoopy dance; Lucy glaring at him, hands on hips.

It seemed unthinkable that a guy wearing such a tie could scare the hell out of me. But he had. I'm not talking your average butterfly. I'm talking I Just Met the Man I Could Imagine Marrying But Can't Because I'm Too In Love With Him.

Ack. I met Noah and his Snoopy tie at a prepublication party for Natasha's memoir, *The Stopped Starlet.* Posh Publishing had gone all out and invited every magazine, newspaper and television show for three hours of high-end drinks, hors d'oeuvres and advance-reading copies of the tell-all memoir. A great many people had shown up, including one Noah Benjamin, a reporter for *Hot News,* a *Times-*meets-*People* weekly magazine. I wasn't a book person; I was a graphic designer, and at the time an unemployed book-cover designer, so while Jane (Natasha's editor), introduced Ethan to her co-workers and schmoozed with the press, and Amanda and Jeff ogled a few celebrities, I stood in a corner popping cheddar-cheese cubes into my mouth.

"Excuse me, I'm a reporter for *Hot News,* and I'd like to ask you a few questions."

Mouth full of cheese, I turned around to find one of the cutest guys I'd ever seen, wearing that red tie with tiny dancing Snoopys and glaring Lucys.

"Um, I'm not anyone," I said like an idiot. "I mean, I'm just a friend of the editor."

He whipped out a tiny notebook and pen. "Name?"

"Eloise Manfred."

He jotted that down. "Favorite food?"

"Um, Mexican."

He jotted that down too. "Favorite type of movie?"

"Romantic comedy."

He tapped his little notebook with his pen. "I'll need your phone number to verify these facts and officially ask you out to a Mexican dinner and a romantic comedy."

Go away. Even the sight of you is giving me heart palpitations.

"I'm on a hiatus from dating," I told him.

"It wouldn't be a date," he said. "It would be an investigation…of our compatibility."

Who could resist? Between the dimple and the tie and the pen tapping on the notebook and that face—that intelligent, sweet, delicious face—I was a goner.

During date one, over black-bean enchiladas, two mango margaritas and an Adam Sandler comedy, I'd fallen in serious like. His cell phone rang six times and he was beeped four times by *Hot News* about a groundbreaking development—a minor celebrity had been spotted walking down Third Avenue on the Upper East Side, shopping in the Gap and Banana Republic and daring to peruse the sale racks. Scandal! We'd spent a fun hour trailing the actress, who yakked on her cell phone the entire time—while walking, trying on clothes, even paying. In Nine West, as she finally put down the phone to try on intricately laced boots, Noah introduced himself as a *Hot News* reporter and asked if he could interview her about her shopping habits. She put on sunglasses and fled with an "Absolutely not!"

There was date two. Three. Four. Seeing each other. A relationship. Casual-serious. An unspoken exclusivity. Living together. But no talk of marriage. Never any talk of marriage.

Until he proposed five days ago.

I'd said yes without hesitation. Three hours later, I was popping Tums in my bathroom. Chewing my cuticles. Having mini-breakdowns in Starbucks with my friends. My ambivalence made no sense. I'd been fantasizing about his asking me to marry him since date number three.

"Yeah, because on date number two, he announced he wasn't ready for a serious relationship," Jane had said when I called to ask if she had any Tums the morning after I'd gotten engaged. "As long as he was noncommittal, you felt safe. He's committed now, and so you're scared to death."

Why? How could I go from wanting to marry Noah more than anything in the world to suddenly wanting things to go back to the way they were before?

Which was wanting him to propose.

Tums, anyone?

"Anyone have a Tums?"

Jane, Amanda and Natasha, sitting next to me on the rim of the sandbox in the Carl Schurz Park playground, dug into their purses, pockets and tote bags. It was unusually warm for early January, almost fifty degrees, and the playground was packed with children in puffy down jackets. Summer was in the sandbox, making Elmo pies from a plastic mold of the Sesame Street character, surrounded by toddlers wielding brightly colored shovels and pails and dump trucks. One little girl was filling her doll's hollow head with sand.

Jane tossed me a bottle of tropical fruit-flavored antacids. I chomped on two as fast I could.

"Me want!" Summer demanded, sticking out her hand at me.

"Sweetie, this isn't yummy. It's yucky!" I grimaced. "Ewwww!"

"Ewww!" Summer repeated. She grabbed a fistful of sand and teased her mother by bringing her hand to her mouth. "Ewww!"

Natasha wagged her finger. "No eating sand. No, no, no."

Summer laughed. "Yes, yes, yes!"

Yes. Yes. Yes. That was exactly what I'd said to Noah when he proposed.

I said yes—three times. So I must have meant yes.

And very soon I was expected to write a five-hundred word article for *Wow Weddings* about *why* I said yes. *Why I Said Yes!* was a regular monthly feature in the magazine, another of Astrid's brainstorms for increasing readership. The articles were written sometimes by celebrities but often by ordinary people about why they fell in love and said yes to their marriage proposals. Astrid wanted articles by both Philippa and me to accompany our feature.

Why I Said Yes! by Eloise Manfred.

Blank page. Blinking cursor.

I said yes because…

Blank page. Blinking cursor.

Part of Philippa's job was to weed through the thousands of *Why I Said Yes!* submissions that came in to *Wow* every month, choose three and submit them to the articles editor, who'd select the best one or scrawl a no on all three and send Philippa back to the mail sack. Part of my job was to read the approved column, design a cute graphic to accompany it and choose an interesting quote to bold for a sidebar. Soon after I started at *Wow,* Philippa received a submission from a bride-to-be in Texas named Laura R. (*Wow* was big on initials only for last names.) Laura R. had been seeing her boyfriend for a year when he was called to service for the army and sent off somewhere awful to fight. He proposed to her in a letter on her birthday, and she wrote back one word: YES! He'd sent her a makeshift ring, a piece of scrap metal he'd fashioned to contain a pretty pebble. He never came home from the awful place, and his parents had given her back the YES! letter with the diary he'd been keeping, which described how happy he was that she'd said yes, how he couldn't wait to get the hell out of there to come home to Texas and marry her and start a family.

I'd sobbed through her entire article. That evening, I'd spent hours at home creating a graphic worthy enough to accompany her column. And then Astrid had decided to reject Laura R.'s submission. "It's too depressing," she'd insisted. "*Wow*'s readers want *happy* endings. They're anticipating *happy* endings for themselves. Not war and death."

Astrid also nixed *Yes!* columns by pregnant brides, overweight brides, gay brides, unattractive brides and blue-collar brides (unless they were marrying up).

"*Wow*'s mission is to preserve the fairy tale," Astrid scrawled in red atop the nixed columns. "Fairy tales are about dreams. Not reality. *Wow Weddings* magazine is about dreams."

I dream you disappear! I prayed with closed eyes during editorial meetings or whenever I heard her heels clicking down the hallways of the *Wow* offices. But then I would open my eyes and she'd still be there. Therefore proving herself wrong. *Wow Weddings* was really about reality.

Why I Said Yes! by Eloise Manfred.

Twice in the past week I've said yes, yes, yes without a moment's hesitation when I meant I don't know, I'm not sure, let me get back to you:

When my boyfriend, Noah, proposed marriage.

When my boss, editor in chief of this very loser magazine, offered me a free dream wedding in exchange for selling my soul as Star Trek Bride.

"Just call me Uhura," I moaned to my friends. "I can't wait to see the futuristic gown I'll be walking down the aisle in to a guy I'm not even sure I should be marrying. Lord knows what he'll be wearing. A space suit, maybe."

"Ura," Summer repeated. "Ura. Ura."

She made a new Elmo pie; a little boy, a toddler around her age, came over to inspect it.

I held up my left hand and wiggled my fingers, staring at the beautiful ring I'd thought I wanted so badly. Now all I thought I wanted was to give it back. Why, why, why?

"Eloise, you're just going through the adjustment of living with a guy," Jane had said the morning after Noah popped the question. "And you've got a bad case of commitment jitters. I think you really do love Noah, but *he's* committed now, and so you're scared. It's the opposite of what happened with Serge and that little proposal fiasco."

She was referring to two and a half years ago, when the very nice guy I'd been dating suddenly proposed and I'd said yes because I wanted It so badly—to be loved, to feel safe in the world. But I didn't love Serge and I'd known it. My friends had known it. If I'd told my grandmother about the engagement, she would have plucked the ring off my finger and mailed it back to him.

I was afraid of commitment? Huh?

"Eloise," Jane said, sifting sand through her fingers, "I really think you *did* mean yes. To both Noah *and* the free wedding. I think it's your fear of commitment creating your cold feet, and not your real feelings. I said this before, but I'll repeat it—I think you said yes to the free wedding so that you couldn't easily take that ring off."

But…

"You know what else I think?" Jane said as Summer jumped on her Elmo pie. "I think your sudden Tums addiction has more to do with your *family* than with Noah."

"How about those Mets!" I responded.

"Me out!" Summer said, heading for the shallow steps. She stopped as a man placed a toddler next to her in the sandbox. The little boy put up his arms and said, "Da-da. Da-da."

Summer put up her arms, too, and said, "Da-da."

The man smiled uncomfortably, as every man did when Summer called him Da-da, which she did to every man, everywhere. In elevators, on the street, in restaurants. Every man was Da-da.

"Where Da-da?" Summer asked Natasha, her green eyes curious.

No matter how many times Summer asked Natasha that question, the same strain tightened Natasha's beautiful features. "Your daddy's in California," Natasha replied, as she did every time. And satisfied, as she was every time, Summer continued playing. She climbed out of the sandbox and ran smiling to the slide.

Natasha waited at the end of the slide to catch Summer. "At least I think he is," she whispered to us. "He's not i-n-t-e-r-e-s-t-e-d," she spelled out. She shook her head, then smiled up at Summer. "Come down to Mama!"

The father of Natasha's baby had broken up with her when she told him she was pregnant. His name was Sam and he lived in California, and for reasons I would never understand, he wasn't interested in knowing his child.

How was that possible?

This was a question people had tried to answer in my own life. *Your father was never the settling-down sort. Your father's creative. Your father's this. Your father's that.*

Your father is a piece of shit.

No one ever said that, but a long time ago, I'd begun to think *that* was the reason Theo Manfred had walked out on his family, never to be seen or heard from again.

The problem with that line of thinking was that you didn't want to think of your father as a piece of shit. You wanted to think of him as a hero.

As Summer ran around the jungle gym and back up to the top of the slide with a "Me do! Me do!" and tried to make her way down alone, I wondered what she'd say when people asked where her father was.

Summer, where's your dad?

He's in California.

When's he coming back?

Never.

Why?

He's not i-n-t-e-r-e-s-t-e-d.

Eloise, where's your dad?

I don't know.

Why don't you know?

I never had an answer to that, so in elementary school I started making things up. He's in Alaska, working on the pipeline. He's climbing Mount Everest (that one was my favorite). He's in China, Switzerland, France, California on business.

The two things I never said was that he was dead or that he took off. I didn't want either to be true.

I picked up a fistful of sand and clenched it. "I haven't seen my father since I was five and I haven't spoken to my brother in over a year," I blurted out.

Three pairs of eyes were staring at me.

"Oh, honey," Amanda said, sitting down next to me on the rim of the sandbox. "I didn't know about your father. You never talk about him."

"Now we understand why," Jane said, squeezing my hand. "I'm so sorry, El."

I shrugged, not knowing what to say, how to respond. It wasn't as though I could say, *It's okay.* Something like that wasn't okay and never would be. Not when it happened and not now.

I haven't seen my father since I was five, but it's okay.

Could you imagine a more ridiculous statement?

"I just don't understand it," Natasha said, her eyes on Summer. "I'll never understand it. How does someone leave his own child?"

I shrugged again. "It's too bad the two people who could explain it are MIA."

"I doubt Summer's dad or yours could explain it either," Jane said. "What answer is there for that question? It's not about *not* loving the child."

How did she know? Maybe it was.

"I love you, Elly-Belly," my father had said often.

So was he lying, or is there no answer for why fathers are able to leave their children and never see them again?

"Your father loves you, Eloise," my mother had said many times. "I'm sure he'll always love you. But he's not the sticking-around kind. It isn't about you or your brother or even me. It's about him. Something in him."

"Yeah, it's called not loving me or Emmett."

"No, Eloise. Something might be lacking in him, but it isn't loving you or your brother. I know it's hard to understand now, but it'll get easier when you've been through some stuff yourself."

Well, I'd been through some stuff myself. And under-standing why my father left—left as though he'd never known us at all—hadn't gotten easier.

Natasha handed Summer her sippy cup of juice. "Elo-ise, I didn't even know you *had* a brother."

"We've been on the outs for the past year," I explained, and then burst into tears.

"El, I'm so sorry," Jane said.

Amanda and Natasha nodded sympathetically.

I hadn't even told Jane, whom I usually told everything, about the last time I spoke to Emmett. A year ago, when my grandmother was in the hospital recovering from a stroke, Jane (who'd come every single day bearing fortify-ing treats for me, like bottles of Coca-Cola and M&Ms), had asked why Emmett hadn't visited.

"Because he's a self-absorbed jerk asshole," I'd screamed like a lunatic.

And for the millionth time in our friendship, which was probably the only thing in the world besides my grandmother that I couldn't live without, Jane had slung an arm around my slumped shoulders and off we'd gone to St. Monica's Church to light candles for our losses, our monthly ritual despite the fact that neither of us was Catholic. Jane's father died from a brain aneurysm when she was nine, and her mother died from ovarian cancer, as mine did, when she was nineteen. She understood.

During some of those candle-lightings, when I'd been there more for Jane than myself, I would wonder which was worse: a dead father or a deadbeat father. A father who was taken from you by the fates of the universe, or a father who was taken from you by his own free will.

Jane and I had never had that conversation because I never spoke about my father.

"So was I right?" Jane asked, shaking sand out of her shoe. "Is it possible that what's going on with your cold feet has something to do with your family?"

"I really don't want to talk about it," I said. I couldn't talk about it.

But I was going to have to. Because a month from now, my brother and father were expected in the *Wow* photography studios for a family-photo shoot.

"Are you going to hire stand-ins?" Amanda asked.

I shrugged. "I guess."

Hello, I'm looking for a fake father and a fake brother to stand in for my real father and real brother at a photo shoot. They should wear black T-shirts, and use hair gel for that "urban appeal." No, I don't need to meet them beforehand; the more like strangers they seem, the more like my real family they'll be!

"El-eez sad?" baby Summer asked, peering up at me from her mother's lap, her sandy little hands wrapped around her sippy cup.

I played with her pretty auburn curls peeking out from under her knit hat. "No, sweetie. Eloise happy."

Summer smiled, handed me her Elmo mold and began clapping. "Elmo. Elmo!"

Making Elmo pies with a two-year-old till the sun went down sounded pretty good to me at the moment.

chapter 3

Living with Noah was a lot like living alone, except that I now lived in a very nice one-bedroom brownstone on the Upper West Side, a five-minute walk to Central Park and the Bethesda fountain with its Angel of Waters statue, where I did my best thinking. And, there was his stuff, of course, guy stuff—electric shavers and black Calvin Klein underwear and button-down shirts and big black shoes and gigantic Boston University gray sweatshirts that I put on whenever he left for one of his trips.

As an investigative journalist, Noah was always leaving at a moment's notice for business trips to a scandal-ridden somewhere. One minute he could be brushing his teeth and the next he would be on a plane to L.A. to cover a pop star's fight with her boyfriend, toothbrush still in hand.

This weekend he was in Washington with Ashley, his annoyingly voluptuous co-worker who tended toward tight V-necked sweaters. Apparently, the daughter of a famous politician and her aging rock-star husband were holding a press conference outside her father's office. Noah and Ashley often did a *He Said, She Said* sidebar on the same story, offering each of their thoughts from a gender perspective. In *Hot News* focus groups, their *He Said, She Said* column was rated as a subscriber favorite.

Translation: Noah and Ashley weren't going to be sent to opposite ends of the earth anytime soon.

In my little corner of the world, though, on the sofa that Noah and I bought together, our first major purchase as a couple, was a two-foot-high chocolate Santa with a note: *I love you, fiancée of mine. See you Monday night.—N.*

I shook the sand out of my shoes, picked up my Santa and unwrapped a leg. I was a chocoholic. I loved these awful hollow chocolates that drugstores and supermarkets sold for every possible holiday. Noah had a stash from Christmas to last me until Valentine's Day, when he'd start hoarding giant red-foil-wrapped chocolate lips. Every time he left on a trip, he'd leave me a giant chocolate something with a lovey-dovey note.

I'd rather have Noah. Around. Home.

"I love you too," I said to the empty apartment. "I do, I do, I do."

I did. I changed into his big gray Boston U sweatshirt and inhaled the yummy smell of his soap and aftershave, flopped on the couch, broke off one of Santa's legs and stared at my diamond ring, twinkling in the dim light.

I'm engaged. I'm getting married.

A moment of elation.

Then a dull panic.

I twisted the ring around my finger.

Two days ago on the subway, the total stranger sitting next to me said, "You know what that means, when you twist an engagement ring or a wedding ring around on your finger like you're doing? It means you want it *off*. It means you don't want to get married."

Had I been twisting my ring? I guess I had.

But I didn't want it *off*. Yes, I did. I didn't. I did, I didn't. I did, I didn't.

Didn't.

Noah proposed on New Year's Eve. For hours I'd been sitting next to an empty chair at a nightclub table full of happy couples, and then suddenly, I was engaged.

I tried to remember how I'd felt just moments before Noah had unexpectedly shown up. I was at Celebrate, a nightclub in Forest Hills, Queens, with Jane's wedding party—Jane and Ethan, Amanda and Jeff, Natasha and her new boyfriend Gideon, and Jane's cousin Dana and her husband, Larry. Jane's aunt Ina had bought the tickets (seventy-five bucks a couple) as an engagement gift for Jane. As half of my couple was away on business, I thought I could stay home and watch Dick Clark. But Ina had shelled out a whole seventy-five for me, and so I had to go.

Noah was in Las Vegas with Ashley, on the trail of the politician's daughter who'd supposedly run off to Vegas with the aging rock star. Rumor had it they were planning to say I do at the stroke of midnight in one of the wedding chapels.

While I sipped my champagne, thoughts of Noah and Ashley in a hotel room keeping me stone-cold sober, I had visions of coming home to a blinking light on my answering machine:

Hi, El, it's me, Noah. Um, I'm really sorry, especially for leaving a message like this on the answering machine, but I thought I should tell you that Ash and I just eloped, ourselves. We were here and all, right at the Elvis Presley wedding chapel, and you know I've always had a major thing for Ashley, even though I've denied it vehemently. You'll move out while we're on our honeymoon, won't you?

Deep breath. Deep breath. Deep breath.

Celebrate had been packed to capacity with happy couples blowing noisemakers and talking, laughing, eating, dancing, drinking. Kissing. Lots and lots of kissing. Some even had leftover mistletoe from Christmas.

While everyone smooched, I moved pieces of dinner, rubber chicken cordon bleu and limp, waxy green beans and a hard roll, around on my plate. I was the only one who looked as if she wasn't having any fun.

On my left, Jane and her fiancé, Ethan, were making out. Not obnoxiously. Nicely, actually. Kissing the way people did when they were in love.

On my right, Amanda and her husband, Jeff, were debating whether their children, who had yet to be conceived, should be two or three years apart.

Across the table, Jane's cousin Dana Dreer Fishkill and her husband, Larry, were reciting their New Year's resolutions. "I resolve to love you even more, if that's even possible!" Dana was saying.

Natasha and her very good-looking *All My Children* co-star, whom she'd just started dating, were staring into each other's eyes on the dance floor.

And then there was me, sitting next to…no one.

"Omigod, it's eleven forty-five!" Dana had shouted from across the table. "Fifteen minutes until the new year. Whoo-hoo!"

As Dana whoo-hooed and the couples kissed, I slid lower in my chair, hoping I could slip unnoticed under the table and just hang out there for a while.

"Is this seat taken?" a voice whispered in my ear.

Noah!

I whirled around, and there he was, standing behind me, his brown leather jacket dusted with snow, the scarf I bought him for his birthday last month wrapped tightly around his neck. "But you're in Las Vegas!"

He kissed me. "Actually, I'm right here."

I wrapped my arms around him. Moments later, we were on the dance floor, swaying to Madonna's "Holiday."

"I love you, Eloise," he whispered in my ear.

Ten. Nine. Eight…

"I love you too, Noah." And I did. So much!

Seven… Six… Five…

"I couldn't spend New Year's Eve without you," he said, kissing me.

Four… Three… Two…

When the crowd got to *One,* Noah shouted, "Will you marry me?"

Blink. Pinch me.

I blinked. I pinched myself. He was really here. Asking me to marry him.

And as everyone hooted and hollered and clapped and cheered for the new year, I wrapped my arms around him and said, *Yes, yes, yes!*

Three hours later, I was pacing the tiny bathroom in our apartment, chewing Tums. Chewing my fingernails. Chewing my lower lip.

What the heck had happened?

I bit off a piece of Santa's other leg and flopped onto my stomach on the sofa.

R-ring!

I grabbed the phone, hungry for Noah's voice. But it was Philippa Wills.

"Okay, guess who I am," Philippa said. She cleared her throat. "Does this look like a *traditional* dress to you, Philippa?" she said in a raspy voice. "Eloise, you may choose from *this* rack or *that* rack."

I laughed. "Snap, snap, people!"

"I hate Astrid's guts," she said. "I didn't know you lost your mom. I'm so sorry."

The thing about Philippa Wills was that she was more complicated than anyone would ever guess and she could be very kind. When she was kind, like now, I'd feel bad for dreaming she'd find a new Best Friend From Work.

"You mean Acid," I said.

Philippa laughed. "We're lucky our rings fit her definition of classic and modern. Otherwise, I wouldn't be surprised if Astrid made us change them too."

I glanced down at the ring on my left hand.

Twist On.

Twist Off.

"Your ring is so pretty!" she said. "It's good the band is so thin, a thicker setting would have overpowered the diamond. What is that, a half-carat?"

Find a new best friend from work, Philippa!

"So, Eloise, why won't your father and brother be able to come to the photo shoots?"

Nosy. Nosy. Nosy!

"My father lives really far away," I said, but I had no idea if that was true. I had no idea where Theo Manfred lived. "And my brother is climbing Mount Everest."

I wasn't sure why I'd said that. That wasn't the kind of thing you could lie about and months later say, *Oh, I thought he was.*

"Wow," Philippa exclaimed. "That's cool. My brother

couldn't climb a *hill*." She laughed at her own joke. "Weston is Mr. Wall Street, earning millions."

Weston Wills. He sounded like a guy who earned millions.

I was trying to think of my getaway. Cookies burning in the oven? Other line ringing? Someone at the door?

"Omigod, Eloise, I just remembered why I called you in the first place—do you know if we have to type our wedding planning diary entry?"

"Um, I would think so," I said. Although Philippa did have perfect penmanship, of course.

"Okay," she said. "Thanks, Eloise. Bye!"

I'd forgotten about the wedding planning diary.

Your diary entry should focus on the poignancy of shopping for your bridal party without Mother. It's a strong human-interest point for our readership. Yes, a theme of Mother's unfulfilled dream—to see her little girl married.

I glanced at the photo of my mother on my bedside table, my beautiful mother in her red peacoat.

Be perky! Use exclamation points.

I sat down at Noah's desk and turned on his laptop, grateful to have something to think about other than my roiling stomach.

Dear Wedding Diary

Today I went bridesmaid-dress shopping! My brides-maids will be wearing the ugliest dress—if you can even call it a dress—that the world has ever seen! And the world will see it, because my bridal party has been photographed oohing and aahing over it in a national magazine!

Then again, who really reads Wow Weddings!

I felt much better.

★ ★ ★

At 2:00 a.m. on Sunday, I woke up from a nightmare. Astrid O'Connor was my mother and she was taking me wedding-gown shopping in It's Your Day, but it wasn't It's Your Day, it was Saks Fifth Avenue, my mother's favorite department store.

"Does that look like a classic dress to you, Eloise?" Astrid snapped as I ran to a live model wearing the Big Bird dress. "As *Wow Weddings*'s Classic Bride, you must choose a *traditional* dress. How about this lovely Audrey Hepburn-esque gown? Oh, yes, you would look so beautiful in it. I would be so proud to see you walking down the aisle to Noah in this gown."

"But I'm not the Classic Bride. I'm Today's Modern Bride."

Astrid laughed. "Eloise, don't be silly. There's nothing modern about you."

I ran to the model wearing the Big Bird dress, but she backed away, her yellow feathers ruffling. The more I ran, the farther back she went, leaving feathers in her trail.

Suddenly, I was in the dressing room with Mini-Astrid and Jane and Noah and baby Summer holding out her arms and shouting "Da-da. Da-da!"

Astrid drew aside the curtain. "Your wedding planning diary is not in my in-box, Eloise," Astrid shouted. "You cannot get married!" She grabbed my hand and tried to twist off my ring.

Nooooo!

I darted up in bed, my heart pounding, and grabbed Noah's pillow and held it to my chest.

Deep breath. Deep breath. Deep breath.

Astrid O'Connor as my mother? *What?* Why hadn't I paid attention to Psych 101?

I turned on my bedside lamp and sat up in bed, staring up at the ceiling. The dream started to fade, and all I could remember was that Astrid O'Connor was my mother and that I wanted to wear the Big Bird gown but couldn't.

Astrid O'Connor as my mother was a lot more of a nightmare than wearing that yellow feather dress would ever be.

I glanced at the photo of my mother on my bedside table. She was sitting on a bench in Central Park on a gorgeous fall day four months before she died. The trees were changing colors, and a squirrel was racing along the bench next to her.

She'd been happy that day, feeling better than usual, but a good friend's daughter was getting married that night, and my mother wasn't well enough to go. She wanted me to go in her place, and I did.

"Weddings are so stupid," I'd said when I got home. "What's the point? All that money, all that time planning, and for what? Men don't stick around anyway."

"Some men do," my mother had said. "Not every man is like your father, Eloise."

My plan was never to get married. I was scared to death of marriage.

But then my mother died, and what scared me changed.

Be perky. Use exclamation points.

Dear Wedding Diary, I typed.

And typed and typed and typed until I woke up at 6:00 a.m., my face pressed into the warm keyboard.

Wow Weddings Memorandum

From: Astrid O'Connor
To: Eloise Manfred
Re: Wedding-Planning Diary Entry #1
Eloise,
See my comments on the attached. The bits about
your mother need perking up. In *Wow Weddings,*
there is no *cancer,* only *serious illness.* There is no
death, only *loss.* Sidenote: I realize you're in the art
dept. and not editorial, so please consult a dictionary
and utilize your spell-checker for your entries. For example, "casket" has only one "t." —AO

chapter 4

"I got an A on my first diary entry!" Philippa squealed, her pink-and-white face looming over the rim of my cubicle on Tuesday afternoon. "I am *so* getting promoted to assistant editor at my next performance review!"

My diary entry had no grade. Apparently, it was so far afield from what Astrid wanted that it didn't even merit a D+ for effort.

"What did you get?" Philippa asked.

I was saved from answering by the ringing of Philippa's phone.

"Philippa Wills, editorial assistant, *Wow Weddings* magazine," she chirped into the receiver. A moment of silence. A happy shriek. "Hi, Parker! I love you too, sweetsums. No, *you're* sweetsums. No, *you* are! Okay, bye, Parkie."

Parker Gersh was not a Parkie.

Philippa's face appeared over my cubicle again. "I'm getting married—and to the greatest guy on earth!" she trilled. "And it's all thanks to you, Eloise! Four months ago, I didn't even have a boyfriend! And now I'm getting married. Whoo-hoo!"

Four months ago, when I thought I'd been having a private telephone conversation with Jane in my cubicle, Philippa had poked her head in the moment I hung up and said, "At least you *have* a love life, Eloise. At least you *have* a boyfriend, even if he's always away on business with whatshername— What *is* her name, his flirty co-worker who's always all over him?"

Did Philippa listen to every phone conversation I had? Apparently so.

"Ashley," I'd said. *But you can call me Ash because I smolder.* Really. I heard her say it twice at Noah's company Christmas party last month.

"That's right, *Ashley.* It's number two on my list of baby names—not that I even have a boyfriend, let alone a husband. Let alone a baby! Hey, which do you like better for a girl—Ashley or Hayley?"

She didn't wait for an answer. After a five-minute monologue on the merits of each name in turn, she sat herself down in my guest chair and told me every detail of her lack of a love life at age twenty-five. I realized the only way to shut her up was to find her someone to date. So a few days later, when Noah returned from his latest trip, I asked him if he knew anyone to set Philippa up with, someone sort of nerdy yet polished. A refined geek. He came up with Parker Gersh, *Hot News*'s managing editor at age twenty-seven. For their first date, the four of us went out for dinner, and four months later Philippa waltzed into work with a two-carat diamond ring from Tiffany's sparkling on her finger.

She insisted she owed her happiness all to me and Noah,

that both of us simply *had* to be in their wedding as bridesmaid and usher. From that moment on, she'd tortured me with what she referred to as my bridesmaidly duty: flipping through bride magazines on our lunch hour, attending the New Brides Expo at the Javitz Center, listening to every single thing Parker Gersh said and did. When I myself came to work with my own ring, she said, "Fabulous! Now we'll be in *each other's* weddings!" (It was then that Astrid happened by, and none too soon, since Philippa had been about to put deposits down on a reception site.)

Just like that, Philippa was one of my bridesmaids. Three or four or ten times a day ever since, she'd dropped by my cubicle to talk wedding, and I'd gleaned that she wasn't close to her family and had no girlfriends. None. My girlfriends were, outside of my grandmother, the most important people in the world to me. I didn't know what I'd do without them. I couldn't imagine what it would be like to have no friends. Had Philippa not gone to high school? College? Work?

"The Modern Bride and the Classic Bride are wanted in the conference room for a meeting," announced Astrid's assistant.

Philippa's face disappeared. I could hear her shoes clicking in the hallway as she ran.

When I walked into the conference room, I had to blink. Twice. Where was I? The set of a horror movie?

One end of the room had been turned into a dominatrix's parlor. The other end was pure Laura Ashley. Both ends were clearly created out of Astrid's office furniture.

Philippa sat on a tall-backed toile-covered chair beside a lace-covered table. She was ogling the two wrapped gifts on the table. Behind her was a backdrop of a living room.

A fake window with blue-and-white-checked curtains. Wood furniture, heavy on the Americana. A vase of sun-flowers. A bookcase with…quelle surprise, the classics. *Portrait of a Lady* was prominent.

At the other end of the room was Astrid's bloodred leather ottoman. Propped behind it was another back-drop featuring the living room of a vampire's New York City penthouse. The walls were painted gunmetal. There was one window, with a drawn shade that looked to be made of aluminum foil. A sofa, seemingly made of concrete. A coffee table made entirely of Popsicle sticks.

"Eloise, please seat yourself in the Modern Bride's dwelling," Astrid said.

"Which one is it?" I asked, but no one even cracked a smile.

I sat on the leather ottoman. Next to it was Astrid's tray table, imprinted with a subway map of New York City, upon which sat two boxes wrapped in smiley-face paper.

Astrid clapped once. "I've come up with a brilliant pro-motional campaign for the Today's Bride feature."

There were awed whispers of "just brilliant" from her minions.

"We'll run promos in the April and May issues with a photo shoot of the Classic Bride and the Modern Bride opening two engagement gifts in their homes, allowing the *Wow* readership a personal glimpse inside your private worlds."

People were going to think I lived here? I thought, eyeing the metal walls and Popsicle-stick coffee table.

"Readers will be invited into your homes to share in the experience as you each open two gifts," Astrid con-tinued. "One that suits your personality and one that doesn't. You'll smile for the gift that suits and you'll fa-cially express your displeasure at the one that doesn't."

Oh, brother.

Devlin eyed me and let out a disgusted breath. "Some-body fix Eloise's hair—it's too bouncy today. Press it more against her head."

The beauty editor ran over and pressed the sides of my hair against my ears. "Much more modern," she affirmed before flitting away.

"I want it flatter," Devlin ordered, shaking his head. "Let's start with the Classic Bride." He turned his atten-tion to Philippa. "I want to capture you looking at the gifts with pure excitement."

"Yet not greedy excitement," Astrid interjected. "The Classic Bride appreciates the tradition of gift giving, yet she is humble."

Philippa wasn't. She ogled her gifts with the intensity I reserved for chocolate.

"*Not* greedy, Philippa!" Devlin shouted. She toned it down, and he shot a Polaroid. He and Astrid studied it, moved Philippa's seat and table a bit to the left (she was slightly blocking the row of classic books on the back-drop), and then Devlin shot a couple of rolls of film. "Okay, now I want you to open the silver-wrapped pres-ent and beam with joy when you see what's inside."

Philippa grabbed it and ripped open the gift, but she didn't beam.

"I said to beam with joy!" Devlin scolded.

"But it's an iron," Philippa pointed out. "It's hard to beam at an iron. And I've already got one, a good one—"

"Philippa, now we have to waste valuable working time

rewrapping the iron," Astrid cut in with a frown. She snapped, and her assistant grabbed the iron and made quick work of the beautiful wrap job. "Again, Philippa."

Philippa reopened the gift and fake smiled.

She was supposed to "facially express" slight dismay as she opened the next gift, touching her hand to her heart with an "oh my" expression. But when Philippa saw the kitschy wineglasses with tiny cartoon kissy couples hand-painted, she squealed with delight. "I love these!"

They were cute, but nothing you'd want to drink wine out of.

"Philippa, you are supposed to show *displeasure* at the wineglasses," Astrid said. "They are not a traditional gift that befits the taste of the Classic Bride. Get it?"

One Astrid snap later and her assistant was rewrapping the wineglasses.

Philippa unwrapped the glasses again—and giggled with delight.

Astrid glared at her. Devlin sighed with disgust. "Let's move on to the Modern Bride," Astrid said, continuing to glare at Philippa.

I was instructed to open the smaller of the two gifts on my table and flash a huge smile. I unwrapped and frowned. Inside were two more of the cartoon wineglasses that Philippa adored.

Devlin slapped his hand against the table. "Eloise, you're supposed to smile!"

But I hate these stupid glasses!

Astrid snapped. I reopened. I smiled as best I could.

I did well with the gift I was supposed to sneer at. A gold-plated mini-broom and dustpan set, it looked exactly like the one Dottie Benjamin had sent a couple of days ago as an engagement gift with a little note:

Dear Noah and Eloise,
  I told everyone "no gifts" at the engagement party I'm hosting next weekend, but how could I not send my little boy and his bride-to-be a "small something" to get rid of all those dust bunnies? You're not the "Modern Bride" for nothing, El. Hee-hee—just kidding! See you this weekend, Love, Mom and Dad Benjamin

I'd torn up the card in a hundred tiny pieces and threw the stupid mini-broom and dustpan in the garbage can. An hour later, I pulled them out (it took me an hour to pick off the coffee grounds and stewed tomatoes), just in case Mrs. Benjamin needed to sweep something up during a visit. And she did like to visit. And sweep dust bunnies out from under the sofa.

"That was great, Eloise," Devlin said. "Let's get another of you holding the broom by the handle as though it were a dead raccoon."

What?

Apparently, that was the expression on my face at the moment, because Devlin began clicking away.

Wait a minute! "No!" I told him. "You can't put this in the magazine! I received this exact broom set from my mother-in-law-to-be!"

Devlin chuckled. "That's quite funny, actually. I'm sure your future mother-in-law has a sense of humor."

All the women in the conference room turned to stare at Devlin with *you're definitely not married* eyes.

Dottie Benjamin did not have a sense of humor. What she had was a warped point of view.

The day after I moved into Noah's apartment, his parents had come over for our housewarming with resigned expressions and a droopy spider plant. "Herbert and I are *traditionalists,* dear," Mrs. Benjamin had said. "We don't be-lieve in living together. Even if you eventually marry, it's not the same. Anyway, in my day, a man didn't buy the cow when he got the milk for free. So if you did marry, you'd still be a free cow."

That's almost verbatim, really.

My grandmother had a good laugh over that entire ep-isode. "There's nothing wrong with living with a man, marriage or no marriage," Grams had said. "If I'd tested out your grandfather before saying my vows, I might have run for the hills."

Thank God for my grandmother.

"Devlin, it's not funny," I yelped. "She'll think I'm mak-ing fun of her gift!"

As Devlin slipped his camera into its case, Astrid said, "Eloise, there's a reason neither you nor Philippa have photo approval—if we let you pick and choose every lit-tle photo, nothing would be printed. You'd say you looked fat or that your hair looked too brassy or that you had something in your teeth."

Oh, God. Oh, God. Oh, God.

This was so much worse than handing over control to bossy relatives. I'd handed over control to a bossy...boss.

In my in-box, as though it were one of *Wow*'s to-the-circular-file memos about wasting copy paper or a warn-ing that lunch was one hour, not one hour and fifteen minutes, was the Modern Bride's Wedding Plans Sched-ule.

I picked up the three-page packet, closed my eyes, took a deep breath and started reading.

Oh, God. Oh, God. Oh, God.

I was getting married on February 29.

Take head, thump on desk. Hard. Repeat.

Why did this year happen to be a leap year? Why, why, why?

Modern Bride's Wedding Date: February 29: Marrying on a day that comes only once every four years is a truly modern thing to do.

Take head, thump on desk. Again.

My friends were wearing rubber dresses to my wedding, the anniversary of which I would celebrate only every four years.

February 29 was two months from now. Less than two months, really.

It could take me eight weeks alone to work up the guts to tell Astrid that my bridesmaids were not wearing rubber to my wedding. That I wasn't getting married on leap year. That they weren't running that photo of me grimacing in pain over the mini-broom and dustpan set.

With one eye opened, I read the rest of the schedule.

Wedding-gown shopping: *For photographs, please bring along one of the following: a mother, a grandmother or your maid or matron of honor. Eloise, as the Modern Bride, if you have a gay male friend, you may substitute him. Note: Veil and other accessories to be chosen as well.*

Rings: *Please have your groom available for this shoot.*

Caterer: *Please have groom available.*

Registry: *Please have older family member available.*

Honeymoon: Modern Bride and Classic Bride only.

Invitations: *Personal guest list of no more than fifty people (advertisers will be invited, of course) by February 1.*

Thump head on desk. Harder, this time. Repeat.

I couldn't bear to read further.

When I lifted my head, an addendum had been added to my in-box.

Wow Weddings Memorandum

From: Astrid O'Connor
To: To the Modern Bride and the Classic Bride
Re: Sibling Photo Shoot
Please note that as Devlin is going on vacation the last week of January, your sibling-photo shoots have been moved up to Monday. If your siblings cannot attend, please hire the appropriate stand-ins, reimbursable at *Wow Weddings*'s standard, not industry standard. —AO

Translation: If you hire someone really good-looking, you'll have to pay the difference between the averagely good-looking models we use and the gorgeous models other magazines shell out big bucks for.

Mini Flirt Night Round Table Discussion 1,000,000: Which Fake Father and Brother Look Most Like Eloise?
During our lunch hour on Friday, Jane and Amanda and I headed to Perfect People, the model agency *Wow* used. We sat in the reception area, poring over huge leather binders filled with eight-by-ten glossies of men, men and more men. There were gorgeous men. Average men. Ugly men. Tall, short, medium. With hair. Without. With potbellies. Without. (There was even a book labeled Ugly Men Without Hair and Potbellies. According to the Perfect People associate who handed us the books, ugly men without hair and potbellies were in demand for "reality-based" commercials and "before" shots for print ads.)
I asked for the Men With Urban Appeal book. Jane, Amanda and I were each handed a stack of four. There were six books of men over thirty-five with urban appeal, and six under thirty-five. We also received the celebrity look-alike book. *Wow Weddings* had been sued

three times by celebrities who claimed the magazine had hired models of their likeness to sell products they wouldn't endorse. *Wow Weddings* won each time and continued the practice.

Jane was flipping through the look-alike book. "Ooh-la-la—check out Ewan McGregorly!" She slid out the photo and held it up. A label along the border indicated that his name was indeed Ewan McGregorly. The back of the photo listed his vital stats and real name: Harold Flubman. Jane laughed. "Ewan looks like he could be your brother, Eloise." She kissed the photo. "Oooh, he's so hot!"

"Ewan or the model?" Amanda asked.

Jane blew another kiss at Ewan. "Both."

"Well, he isn't supposed to be hot," I pointed out. "He's supposed to be my brother."

"Your brother *is* hot," Jane said.

"Jerks aren't hot," I countered. "They're just jerks."

Jane closed the book and sat down on the sofa next to me. "What happened between you and your brother, anyway?"

I bit my lip, stared at the ceiling, kicked my toe against the beige carpet.

"Does it have something to do with your grandmother and her stroke last year?" Amanda asked.

I bit my lip and fidgeted.

"Eloise, I don't know what happened between you and Emmett," Jane said. "You never told me. I just know that when your grandmother was recovering from the stroke in the hospital, he never came to see her. I also know that you haven't spoken to him since. And that's way too long."

"I don't want to talk about it," I said.

"Honey, you're at a modeling agency to hire a stand-in

brother for a photo shoot of your wedding plans," Jane said. "But you *have* a brother."

"Where is he, then?" I asked. "I also have a father, but I haven't seen him in twenty-seven years. What the hell is the difference?"

"The difference is that until a year ago, you were nuts about your brother," Jane said. "I know he drove you a little crazy, but I also know how much he means to you. I know you've been very protective of him your entire life. And I know that you love him to pieces."

"Call him, Eloise," Amanda said.

I fidgeted, still staring up at the ceiling.

"Will you call him?" Jane asked.

Blank page. Blinking cursor.

"Eloise?"

"Maybe I should just back out of the whole thing," I said.

Jane raised an eyebrow. "Out of a free hundred-thousand-dollar wedding?"

"Out of everything," I said. "The engagement, the wedding, everything."

"Don't make this about Noah when it's not," Jane told me.

"Meaning?" I asked.

"Meaning, this is about you and your feelings about your father and your brother. It's not about Noah. Don't hurt what's there and working."

"Maybe Noah and I *aren't* working. Maybe I want a husband who's around more than twice a week."

"And maybe you want a husband who you love very much," Amanda said. "A husband who loves you very much."

Jane nodded. "And a husband who does quite inadvertently push buttons that force you to deal with stuff."

I shook my head. "I don't want to deal with stuff. I just want to—"

"Bury your head in the sand?" Amanda finished for me.

Was that what I was doing? If you didn't deal with something that you couldn't deal with, were you a big fat ostrich?

Jane squeezed my hand. "Eloise, I'm just saying that the fates of the universe have conspired against you—or for you, actually. You've got to produce a father and brother for your wedding feature. *One* of them is in your life— okay, he hasn't been this past year. But you can remedy that."

"Does your grandmother have his phone number?" Amanda asked.

I nodded.

"Call him, El," Jane said.

I shook my head.

"Call him," she said again.

Call.

Don't call.

Call.

Don't call.

Ah. The fates of the universe had conspired again and landed on Don't Call.

Two minutes later, I had a fake brother named Ewan McGregorly signed, sealed and available for delivery on Monday.

chapter 5

Whereas I had three relatives, one AWOL since I was 5 and one I hadn't spoken to in a year, Noah Benjamin had a cast of thousands. I tried to imagine Thanksgiving dinner with his family.

Pass the turkey, please.

Sorry, it weighs four hundred pounds. Self-serve!

At least a hundred people were stuffed into Noah's parents' New Jersey house for our engagement party. There were siblings, first, second and third cousins, aunts, uncles, grandparents and close friends of the family who were called Aunt This or Uncle That. There were children, at least ten, of various ages, building things out of Play-Doh or reading comic books or sulking about "this stupid boring party." There were even two dogs, a German shepherd named Buddy and a terrier named Scruffy, playing teeth-tug-of-war with a ratty bone.

And there was Noah, looking incredibly handsome in

his gray shirt and charcoal pants, debating the last presidential election with his uncles.

Last but not least, there I was, facing the bookshelves (heavy on the leather-bound editions of classics, à la Philippa's fake library) at the far end of the living room, sipping a glass of wine and staring at my watch, which *tick-tick-ticked* very slowly. It was only seven-thirty. Snippets of twenty different conversations went on around me. Mostly *about* me.

"I hear both her parents are dead, poor thing."

"Nah, Eloise just doesn't talk to her family."

"She's very pretty, but a little skinny, don't you think?"

"Is Uncle Jeffrey coming?"

"Some big advertising promotion for the magazine she works for."

"Maybe her father's in prison. Some kind of white-collar crime, most likely."

"Beth says the bridesmaids have to wear Halloween costumes."

"Can someone *please* turn down the stereo?"

"I thought we were meeting Eloise's family."

"No family?"

"I hear she has a sister."

"No, a brother."

"Eloise has no family—no one. So sad."

"Hmm, this chopped liver is delicious!"

"She has a sickly grandmother. I hear the poor little old lady is in a nursing home."

You hear wrong. You all hear wrong. My grandmother wasn't sickly and didn't live in a nursing home. Five feet ten inches tall and weighing one hundred and seventy-six pounds, seventy-nine-year-old Bette Geller, of the cashmere sweater sets, heavyweight dungarees, rouge and lipstick, was as robust and full-of-life as you got, despite the partial paralysis that made it difficult for her to get around or travel, which was why she wasn't here tonight. She played poker and adored Rodney Dangerfield and hooted with laughter at his movies.

It was true that my grandmother had been sick. A little over a year ago, she'd had a stroke. One minute she'd been fine, sitting across from me in the diner where I met her for lunch every Saturday afternoon, and the next minute, she wasn't fine.

She'd been sipping the chocolate egg cream that she always got for dessert and telling me a joke, one of her favorites of Rodney's that embarrassed her and delighted her at the same time, when she suddenly *stopped,* just sort of froze, and things had gotten worse from there.

There was a rush of waiters, people sitting around us, the diner manager, and then the ambulance sirens. Then there were doctors and nurses and Jane and Amanda and Natasha, baby Summer cooing in her stroller. There was Noah, whom I'd been dating somewhere between casually and seriously for almost a year. There was my old boss at Posh Publishing, a couple of girlfriends from high school and one from college. Even Michael, my ex-boyfriend from a decade before, showed up in the hospital with a bouquet of red tulips and a box of Whitman's Samplers, which my grandmother had kept on her shiny mahogany coffee table every day of the year. There were my grandmother's friends, who'd come every day and sat for hours, playing cards by her bedside, talking to her, telling her who was having a sale on rib roast, whose husband was in the doghouse, whose granddaughter just had a baby.

There was no Emmett, but no one asked why.

It was understood that Emmett was *traveling.*

My brother was one of those "march-to-their-own-drummer" types who graduated (barely) from Yale, then got a job driving a truck to Alaska, where he fished for a while until he decided to climb a mountain in Africa, funding for which was provided by the occasional wealthy older woman he was sleeping with.

I was the only one who asked where Emmett was.

"Where the hell is Emmett?" I'd scream and rage at the top of my lungs in the tiny studio apartment I lived in at the time.

"Jesus Christ, I don't know!" shouted back the guy who lived in the apartment above me. The walls, floors and ceiling in that dumpy walk-up were so thin, you could hear way too much of what went on in your neighbors' lives. I mourned for the days, the years, when Jane lived above me. Before she moved into a swanky Upper West Side apartment with Ethan, Jane and I could conduct entire conversations via our kitchen cabinets.

Where the hell is Emmett? I started raging silently.

Despite the many warm, caring people, from friends to doctors to co-workers to strangers I met in the hospital elevator and in the hallways where I prayed that my grandmother wouldn't die, there was no family.

My family was Grams, myself and Emmett, and Emmett was nowhere to be found.

He often took off for weeks at a time and couldn't be reached.

"What if something happens!" I had yelled at him for years. "You have to be reachable!"

"What's going to happen?" he'd say. "Stop being so melodramatic."

"Get a cell phone!" I'd scream.

"Stop telling me what to do!" he'd scream back. "And I'm not getting a cell phone. You can get cancer from cell phones."

"What if something happens?" I yelled again.

His response was some indecipherable mutter (his usual response).

And then something happened. And I couldn't reach Emmett.

Despite all the people, there'd been no family.

No family meant me. And I was strong, I'd been born strong apparently, and made stronger just a few years later, but I wasn't *that* strong. I wasn't immune to the aforementioned raging. The crying jags, the fear.

Emmett turned up three weeks and four days after my grandmother's stroke, with an overnight bag slung over his shoulder, his stupid grin and shaggy blondish-brown hair that always needed a cut but always looked rock-star good anyway. I opened my apartment door to find him with a girlfriend in tow, a pretty blonde with braided pigtails despite her age, which had to be at least twenty-five. Her name was Charlotte. Emmett wanted to know if he and Charlotte could crash on my couch for a few days until Charlotte's freshly painted living-room walls dried.

"It's a really cool plum color," Charlotte said.

I ignored her and told my brother to go to hell.

"You have a lot of rage," Charlotte said before I clued them both into *why*.

"I didn't know, okay?" he screamed back, red-faced. "How was I supposed to know that Grams had a stroke if I didn't know?"

Gee, Emmett, and you went to Yale?

"You were supposed to know because you should have

been here!" I said. "You should have been here or should be reachable. But you're a selfish, self-absorbed brat!" I stood there yelling. "Grams is all we have of family… where the hell have you been since you were eighteen… taking off on whims without a second thought…leaving all the responsibility to me…where have you been the past three weeks when Grams, our only family in the world, has been in a hospital, slowly recovering from a stroke that you didn't even know she had…you wouldn't know it if I dropped dead in the street… Selfish brat!… Self-absorbed!… Immature!…"

I went on and on and on.

Lips tight, Emmett listened until I stopped yelling. Then he said, "I don't need this crap," and he and Charlotte stomped off, her pigtails flopping against her puffy white jacket as they headed down the stairwell.

That was the last time I saw him.

He sent my grandmother postcards. During the past year, he'd been all over the United States. Beverly Hills. Las Vegas. Chicago. Nashville and Memphis. Atlanta.

"Don't be so hard on your brother," Grams would say when I'd toss the postcard aside with a *harrumph*. "It's all very complicated."

It wasn't complicated. Nothing was complicated. Things either were or weren't.

And Emmett was a weren't.

"Emmett and I have the same background," I ranted to Grams. "What's complicated about him should be complicated about me. And here I am!"

"Yes," she'd say, "but you're different people."

Right. I was a normal human being who took care of the one true relative aside from Emmett I had on this earth. And Emmett was a self-absorbed jerk brat!

"Things aren't black and white, dear," Grams would say.
I would nod, but I secretly didn't agree.

You were or you weren't.

"Eloise, dear, as a traditionalist…"

Startled out of the memories, I turned around to find Noah's mother, Dottie Benjamin, eyeing me with a frown. I took my hand off the leather-bound *Great Expectations* I didn't even know I was clutching.

"Dear," Mrs. Benjamin said, "I'm sure Beth was exaggerating—she's been in the foulest mood lately—but she was muttering like crazy about having to wear a Halloween costume to her own brother's wedding. Dear, does that make any sense to you? I couldn't make heads or tails of it."

A woman standing behind Mrs. Benjamin wiggled her way through the small group of people between us. "Louise, did I just hear that you and Noah are marrying on Halloween—in costume? How festive!"

Eloise, I corrected mentally. Why waste the breath? Besides, the woman was already deep in conversation about whether Cousin Marcy was carrying high or low and whether that meant she was pregnant with a boy or a girl.

I turned back to my future mother-in-law. "Mrs. Benjamin, the dress is a little different, but—"

Mrs. Benjamin leaned close. "Dear, a wedding is no time for *different*. But don't you worry—I saw the most beautiful bridesmaid dress today, and I took it upon myself to put a deposit on five of them. Don't even try to thank me—that's what a mother-in-law is for! The dress is a lovely deep purple taffeta with cute little polka-dot bows on the neckline and a festive bow at the back waistline. Beth, as you know, looks great in jewel tones."

"Um, Mrs. Benjamin, the magazine feature—"

She waved her hand. "Oh, don't you worry about a thing! Once your boss sees these dresses, I'm sure she'll want to feature them in the magazine."

"Mrs. Benjamin—" I waited for her to say, *Dear, call me Dottie, we're family,* but she never did. "I hope you can get back your deposit. The bridesmaids' dresses are a done deal. Yes, they're a little different, but—"

"Different?" repeated Beth, appearing out of nowhere behind very pregnant cousin Marcy. "It's *hideous.* I'm not wearing it. I'm a size fourteen if you haven't noticed, and there's no way that skintight thing will look good on me."

Be kind, she's going through a divorce, I mentally chanted.

"The color's great on you, though," I said.

Mrs. Benjamin and Beth Benjamin eyed me as though I were speaking Swahili, as they often did at family functions.

Two of the kids began feeding the little dog Play-Doh, and Mrs. Benjamin ran off to save it. Beth slunk away, and I was back to my books and inability to shut out conversations about me.

"I hear they're getting married on Halloween."

"Their wedding is a costume party."

"What? What kind of nonsense is that?"

"It's bad luck is what it is!"

"Ooh, I'm going to go as Jay Leno. I bought a rubber mask of his face last year."

"I just met Eloise's mother. Lovely woman."

I raised my eyebrow at that one. What I would do to meet my mother at this party, chat with her for a little while. Hear her voice. The voice of reason, at that.

"We can sneak out if you're dying," Noah whispered in my ear. "There are so many people here, no one will notice."

Effectively reminding me of why I had said yes all over again.

Sunday morning, Noah and I got into a huge fight.

"You're mad at me because I drank the last of the Diet Coke?" he asked.

I stood in the doorway to the bedroom, waving the empty soda bottle at him. "Whoever drinks the last of the soda has to either buy more or write *Buy More Soda* on the fridge!"

"Fine. I'm sorry. I will."

"Oh, like you can buy soda from Chicago," I snapped.

"What?"

"Stay home," I said. "Blow off the trip. Who cares if Oprah is rumored to be marrying Steadman in a secret ceremony on air?"

"Eloise, I can't *not* go," he said. "It's my job."

Sometimes I wanted his job to be being my fiancé.

"Are you mad that I drank the last of the soda or that I'm going away?"

"That you're going away," I admitted, and slunk down on a chair like a sulking child.

He sat down next to me. "Sweetie, being an investigative journalist means hitting the road. I'm very likely going to be traveling a lot forever."

But—

"Eloise, I know it's hard on us as a couple, but I love you and you love me and—"

"'We're a happ-y fam-i-ly'?"

"What?"

Noah didn't do much baby-sitting for two-year-olds and have the preschool crowd's theme songs down pat.

"I'll be all right," I said. "I've just got a lot on my mind."

"If you need me, Eloise," he said, "you just call me." He took my hands and looked into my eyes. "You come first. You need me and I'm in the middle of interviewing Oprah's friend's friend's cousin's next-door neighbor's sister, I'll take your call. You can count on that."

I hit him with a pillow.

But I did feel better.

"So are you going to call Emmett?"

I didn't feel better.

"Give it some thought," he said.

I nodded and watched him choose between his red Snoopy tie and his blue Addams Family with tiny Morticias. He added Morticia to his at-the-ready duffel bag, the one that was always packed and ready to go at a moment's notice, then kissed me long and hard and passionately, and was gone.

Call Emmett. Don't call. Call Emmett. Don't call.

I spent my Sunday going back and forth, back and forth.

When the sun went down, I moved from the couch to my bed and grabbed my packet from Perfect People. I pulled out the photo of my fake brother, Ewan McGregorly. He had long teeth. Model's teeth.

I smiled wide at myself in the mirror over the dresser. I didn't have big teeth. I had my mother's teeth, my mother's smile.

I had my father's eyes. So did Emmett.

Ewan did too, apparently. Well, close enough. Almond-shaped, but slightly turned down at the corners.

Under my bed was a box containing the one photo album that had pictures of my father. I pulled the album onto my bed and flipped through it.

On the second page, Emmett, in his Scooby Doo pajamas, was sitting on Theo Manfred's shoulders, covering his eyes and laughing. Theo was laughing too.

How did you go from being the man in this picture to never seeing that little boy again? Never feeling the weight of that little body in your arms? Never seeing that face, so much like your own?

How?

There was also one of me on his shoulders. *Eloise, age five, and Daddy,* said the caption label that my mother wrote. Theo Manfred's hands were around my ankles, and he was looking up at me. My hands were high in the air, and my smile was so big it must have hurt.

Every time I looked at that picture, I thought that I must have felt safe up there.

Look, Ma, no hands.

Again, how? How could you go from this picture to never seeing that little girl again?

The one photograph that always made me feel slightly sick was the one of me, just me, holding a small white paper bag in one hand and a fistful of jelly beans in the other. I was five.

My father had bought me that bag of jelly beans. He used to take me to one of those tiny candy shops lined with plastic cubbies filled with brightly colored candies and silver scoops. He'd hand me a white paper bag and check his watch.

"You have exactly one minute and fifteen seconds to fill up this white paper bag with all the candy you want," he'd say. "Ready, set…go!"

And tongue out in fierce concentration, I'd go running. For the Tootsie Rolls. For the chocolate turtles. For the jelly beans. I'd end up with a pound of candy to eat for the week.

A couple of days after he left for good, I found three jelly beans at the bottom of the bag, green ones that I didn't like and couldn't get Emmett to eat, either. I scrunched up the bag and put it under my mattress. When I was thirteen and alternating between apathy and fury that later would become my trademark ambivalence about everything, I threw it away. Emmett, ten at the time, had thrown a fit. *You should have given the bag to me...I don't have a last thing from our father...who do you think you are, Eloise! I hate you! I hate everybody!*

I'd changed in that instant. I'd gone from being your basic self-absorbed new teenager, wondering why I didn't have my period, to being aware of people's feelings. Suddenly, Emmett wasn't my younger brother, in turn annoying and funny; he was a deeply sad boy whose father had left before he even had a chance to know him. I became ferociously protective of Emmett. If a bully was bothering him, I stalked over, hands on hips. If Emmett crumpled up his math homework in frustration because of not being able to do his fractions, I uncrumpled the loose-leaf paper and explained what a lowest common denominator was. If I was locked in my bedroom, devastated that a boy didn't like me and heard Emmett howling with laughter over Saturday-morning cartoons, I smiled.

Once, I asked my mother if there was something wrong with me for caring so much about Emmett, when my friends wished their siblings would take a rocket to Mars.

"Loving your brother is one of the best things you can possibly do," my mother had said.

I grabbed the phone and punched in Emmett's telephone number. After the *You know what to do* recording, I said, "Look, I'm getting married and I need you to show up for a photo shoot I'm doing for *Wow Weddings.*" I rambled on for a minute, then said, "So if you can come, great, and if you can't, that's okay too. Whatever."

chapter 6

On Monday morning, Emmett Manfred was sitting in the reception area of *Wow Weddings,* reading a battered paperback copy of *Ulysses.* The receptionist, Lorna, was staring at him. Salivating over him at 9:00 a.m. as though he were a bagel and cream cheese and a cup of strong coffee.

The bagel and cream cheese will last longer, I wanted to tell her.

"Eloise, your brother is here to see you," Lorna said.

"I see. Thanks."

He needed a haircut. His sandy-brown hair flopped in his eyes, which were huge and golden-hazel and both puppy dog and penetrating.

Relief sagged through me at the sight of him. This past year, I knew he was okay, that he wasn't dead in a ditch somewhere, that he wasn't begging for change on a street corner or selling his body or involved with loan sharks or anything else I might have seen on *Law and Order.* I knew from the tone of the postcards he sent to my grandmother that he was absolutely fine.

But here my baby brother stood, alive and well and his usual self, wearing a Jimi Hendrix T-shirt and frayed jeans and a very expensive-looking brown leather jacket.

He nodded at me, put *Ulysses* in the messenger bag slung around his torso and stood up. "So I'm here."

"I see," I said again.

We stepped toward each other in an awkward *should we make some kind of physical gesture* movement? then decided being in the same room was, for the moment, enough.

"Do you need somewhere to stay?" I asked. "Money?"

"I'm just here, okay? No big deal."

"Fine."

"Fine."

Astrid came sweeping into the office, her assistant and Mini-Astrid at her heels. I introduced Emmett.

Astrid smiled a smile usually reserved for strong circulation numbers. "Lovely to meet you, Emmett. You're everything the Modern Bride's brother should be."

"That's quite a compliment coming from you," he drawled, as though he were from Texas or had any idea who she was.

Triple eyeroll.

She smiled and gave him an official once-over. "I don't want Devlin to change a thing. You are absolutely perfect as is for the shoot. Come, let me show you around our offices."

As Emmett flashed his dimples and opened the inner door for Astrid like the gentleman he wasn't, I ran to my cubicle, called Perfect People and canceled my fake brother.

★ ★ ★

Wow rented space in a photography studio on West Seventeenth Street. Emmett and I shared a cab and didn't say a word to each other. He looked out his window; I looked out mine.

"Thanks for coming, by the way," I finally said.

He glanced at me and nodded.

"Do you remember Noah?" I asked him. "My fiancé? You met him a couple of times at Grams's."

"Tall guy, right? Smart. Likes spinach."

"That's Noah," I said, smiling at the memory of his having two helpings of my grandmother's spinach despite the fact that he hated green vegetables.

"So what do I have to do at the photo shoot?" Emmett asked.

"The photographer will direct you," I said. "You just smile a lot, basically."

He nodded. "Your boss thinks I could be a model. She said so while she was showing me around the offices."

"She knows what she's talking about," I told him. "She's the editor in chief. She could hook you up with the agency we use at *Wow.*"

"I'd never sell out like that," he muttered. "Like I want a bunch of assholes to go buy five-hundred-dollar shirts because of me?"

"You'd *make* five hundred dollars just to wear that shirt for an hour," I pointed out.

"I'd rather earn my money the hard way."

"How *do* you earn your money?" I asked him.

"This and that," was his response.

This was very likely having sex with wealthy older women and *that* was probably waiting tables in trendy restaurants to meet them in the first place.

"This and that is better than smiling for an hour?" I asked.

"This and that is honest."

"I see," I said.

"No you don't," he responded.

"No, you're right. I don't."

The taxi stopped at our destination, and he pulled out his wallet. "Look at that, we agree about something."

"Put your money away," I told him.

"This and that pays," he said. "I have money."

"It's on *Wow*."

He slid his wallet back into his pocket. "In that case…"

We headed inside the studio and found half the staff of *Wow Weddings* in room three, where it was summertime in the city. A huge bright blue backdrop with fluffy white clouds, a park bench and even a terrier scampering about a tree was in front of one wall. Philippa and a guy who had to be her brother, both of them dressed in summery whites with pink accents for her and blue for him, stood in front of the backdrop, turning this way and that and fake laughing. Her brother kept throwing back his head and fake laughing, his mouth open wide.

"Great, Weston!" Devlin said. "Okay, one more big laugh. Yes, that's it. Move slightly to the left. Philippa, take out a photograph of your fiancé and show it to your brother with a wistful expression."

"Ooh, I have soooo many pictures of Parker," Philippa said. "Which one should I pick?"

"Just pick a good one," Devlin told her.

"As if there could be a bad one," Weston Wills said, tsk-tsking Philippa with a wag of his finger.

Emmett stared at them, clearly waiting for Weston to turn sarcastic. It didn't happen.

Philippa selected a photo from her purse album and showed it to her brother. "Just think, Wes, Parker is going to be your brother-in-law!"

"It's so exciting," Weston said. "Nothing is more important than family, and now our family is expanding."

Emmett was staring at them as though they were from outer space.

"Philippa, point at the photo and beam," Devlin said. "Weston, smile proudly."

They beamed and smiled proudly and Devlin clicked and clicked and clicked.

"Okay, Classic Bride, that's a wrap," Devlin said.

"Excellent, Philippa," Astrid said. "Simply excellent. I couldn't be more delighted."

Philippa beamed and squeezed her brother into a hug. "Yay for us!" she shouted.

I tried to remember the last time Emmett and I hugged. Not in years. He wasn't a hugger; he was more a knuckle-acknowledger, like the Yankees.

The last time we hugged was at our mother's funeral. And that had taken some doing on my part.

Weston was now giving Philippa a piggyback ride around the studio. He looked a lot like Philippa, down to the thick, fine white-blond hair, the dark blue eyes, the perfect complexion, the preppiness. He was as all-American clean-cut as you got.

"I love you, sis," Weston said as they piggybacked over to where the *Wow* crowd was prepping for the Modern Bride's sibling shots.

Did people really say that? *Sis?* Clearly they did.

"You're the best, Philly!" Weston added, giving her long blond hair a little yank.

"No, *you're* the best," Philippa said, slugging him on the shoulder.

Weston pointed a finger at her. "No, *you're* the best."

"No, *you're*— Nope, you're right. I *am* the best!" she said.

He hooted with laughter and chased her around the studio, culminating in catching her and giving her a gentle noogie.

Emmett and I were the only ones who seemed to be paying attention to Philippa and her brother. Was this how all families—with the exception of ours, of course—acted? Did Astrid chase her younger brother or sister around the house at Thanksgiving, giving her noogies until she yelped Uncle?

"Okay, I'll break the tie," said an attractive fiftyish woman as she hopped off a stool by the buffet. "You're *both* the best!"

"Mom!" Philippa exclaimed. "How long have you been here? I wasn't sure you'd be able to make it at all! I thought you were volunteering at the soup kitchen today."

Mrs. Wills smiled. "I left a few minutes early to catch my two babies at their photo shoot. I'll go back tomorrow and make up the time. There's nothing like philanthropy to warm the soul, especially on a chilly winter day," she added.

"Chilly?" Emmett said. "It's seventy-five degrees and sunny. Look—" He pointed at the backdrop of the fake summer day.

The Willses glanced at him curiously.

"Am I too late?" asked a man entering the studio. He had to be Philippa's father. He looked like an older version of Weston, right down to the suit and expertly cut blond hair.

"Daddy!" Philippa gushed, running toward him. "You came! But what about the shareholders' meeting?"

Mr. Wills kissed her on the cheek. "Sweetie, family comes first."

"Oh, Daddy!" Philippa said.

"Group hug!" her mother trilled.

The Wills Four group-hugged. The parents, very attractive, blond, tanned and expensively dressed, with tasteful pieces of gold jewelry, looked as if they'd just stepped out of a Ralph Lauren ad. The Willses were the healthiest-looking people I'd ever seen in my life.

"Our baby girl is a model!" her dad exclaimed. "I always told you you should be in pictures, Philippa."

Philippa fake batted him on the arm and beamed. "Oh, Daddy! I'm not a model. Just a bride."

"Just a bride!" He chuckled. "Just a bride who's saving her daddy a hundred grand. I'll just have to spend the money you're saving me on something else. Like maybe a down payment on a Tribeca loft for my baby girl."

"Really, Daddy? Omigod! I'm moving to Tribeca! Whoo-hoo!"

"You deserve all the happiness in the world, Philippa," her mother said. "I'm so proud of you!"

"My baby sister's done good," Weston Wills said, slinging an arm around her. He glanced at his watch. "Ooh, I'd better hop in a cab. I've got an important meeting in a half hour."

As the Wills Four hugged and kissed goodbye, I watched them—the affection, the love, the pride, the goofiness—and I felt honest-to-goodness one hundred percent jealousy.

I was grateful that Emmett was here. I didn't have parents, but I did have a brother. And for the first time in a year, he was five feet away from me.

★ ★ ★

"Emmett, honey," Devlin said, "you're going to have to—"

Emmett all but put up his dukes. "Yo, buddy, I'm not going to do anything if you call me honey again."

"Testy," Devlin mock chided.

Devlin wasn't gay. He clearly had thought Emmett was, though, and was trying to talk to him in his own language to get the shot he wanted.

"Fine. Emmett nothing," Devlin amended. "You're going to have to uncross your arms and lose the scowl. You're supposed to be happy and proud in these shots. Your sister is getting married."

Emmett dropped his arms.

"Emmett," Devlin snapped, "you're not playing *dead*. You're playing *happy*. Proud. Whoo-hoo, my big sis is getting hitched. Can't wait to cavort with the bridesmaids in their sexy dresses!"

News flash: Devlin, you've seen the bridesmaid dresses. Sexy ain't the word.

Emmett gave me a *Who-is-this-loser?* look.

"Devlin," Astrid intervened with a toss of her wrap over her shoulder. "The Modern Bride's brother can have a semblance of a scowl. After all, a wedding is in itself a traditional event, and a James Dean 'get me out of here' expression would work beautifully for the piece."

I glanced at Emmett, standing by the fake terrier against the brilliant blue backdrop. He wore a black T-shirt and black jeans, a slim leather-strap necklace and the big black boots. I had no doubt that Get Me Out of Here was first and foremost on his mind.

"I'm not petting the dog," Emmett told Devlin.

"Did I ask you to?" Devlin said, spinning a finger by his ear.

"Should I kill him now or wait a few minutes?" Emmett growled.

"Devlin, we mustn't upset the talent," Astrid intervened.

Devlin snorted. "He's not 'the talent'—he's just Eloise's brother."

"Time is ticking," Astrid said, tapping her watch. "Let's continue with the shoot, please."

Devlin and Emmett narrowed eyes at each other for a few seconds, then Devlin instructed me to show Emmett a photograph of "Noel."

"Noah," Emmett corrected for me.

"Whatever," Devlin said.

"No, not whatever," Emmett retorted. "His name is Noah."

Devlin rolled his eyes. "Are we going to argue or are we going to shoot this segment?"

I ran over to my tote bag and pulled out my wallet, which had my favorite picture of Noah tucked inside. He was making a peanut butter and Fluffernutter sandwich in our kitchen.

I showed the photo to Emmett. He glanced at it. "Noah likes Fluff?" he asked. "Now I know he's okay."

"Fabu, Emmett," Devlin said. "More of that expression."

Devlin shouldn't have said anything. Emmett glanced up at him and scowled, and that was that.

Devlin sighed. "Emmett, put your arm around Eloise's shoulder, and, Eloise, throw your head back and hoot with laughter as though he just told you something really funny. Made fun of your dad's ugly eyeglasses or something."

Emmett stiffened, just slightly. Our father hadn't worn eyeglasses.

"Emmett, adopt a teasing expression," Devlin said. "A get-me-out-of-here-but-I-love-you-sis look."

"This is so lame," Emmett muttered.

"Eloise, for God's sake, tell your brother a joke. I can't shoot this if he's going to stand there like a piece of driftwood."

Emmett adopted his I-am-going-to-kill-this-moron look.

"Why did the drummer eat chicken before his concert?" I said to no one in particular. "Because he needed a new pair of drumsticks. Ba-dum-pa!"

Emmett loved that stupid joke—or at least he had when he was a kid. For weeks when he was seven or eight, he insisted I tell it every night before he went to bed.

I had no idea if it would work or backfire. It worked. Emmett smiled.

"A ham sandwich walks into a bar," he countered. "He asks the bartender for a beer. The bartender says, 'Sorry, we don't serve food.' Ba-dum-pa!"

"That's what you two find funny?" Devlin asked, clicking away.

"Where'd you find this bozo?" Emmett whispered. "What a loser."

"I'd agree but I'd get fired," I whispered back.

Emmett and I spent the next five minutes topping each other with jokes. Devlin shot four rolls before Emmett even knew it.

On Saturday, my grandmother hosted a get-to-know-each-other brunch for the two families. Noah's parents and sister came bearing a pound of chopped liver and a box of butter cookies with multicolored sprinkles. Emmett arrived with the pigtailed girlfriend I'd met briefly in my doorway last year.

Interesting. Emmett had never brought a woman

"home" to meet the family. In fact, I'd never met one of Emmett's girlfriends, and now I was seeing this one for the second time—at a family brunch, no less—a year later. Were they serious? Just friends? Had Emmett given up the wealthy older women he used to brag about "dating" for a woman his own age? It was amazing how little I knew of Emmett's personal life.

"Charlotte?" my grandmother repeated when Emmett introduced her.

"Charl*a*," she enunciated. "Like Charlotte but with the *a*. Charla Gould."

"Charla," we all repeated, suspicious of her shoulder-length braided pigtails. She wore a sparkly lavender knit cap, a puffy white down jacket to her knees and white leather knee-high boots with low platform heels. When she took off her coat, we were all surprised by how slight she was. She had on the tiniest miniskirt, red and black and white plaid, and three layers of tiny ribbed long-sleeved shirts. She was very pretty, but she hid it.

"Hmm, is that ruggelah?" she asked, eyeing the dining-room table.

That was all it took for my grandmother to fall for her. Charla and Emmett were the same. Able to charm anyone with just the right question.

Charla ogled the spread on the table. "I love ruggelah! It's good for the soul."

We sat, we filled our plates, we said yes or no to coffee or tea.

"Isn't this nice," my grandmother commented after a couple of rounds about the weather and the traffic on the George Washington Bridge, which, according to Mrs. Benjamin, had been horrendous.

"So, Emmett," Mrs. Benjamin said, heaping chopped liver on a lettuce leaf. "What is it that you do?"

"I think," was Emmett's reply.

Mrs. Benjamin paused. "You think? I don't understand."

"He means a think tank, like they have in Washington," Noah's father said. "Is it true you guys make a fortune for just sitting around talking?"

Emmett raised an eyebrow. "I wouldn't know. I just think for myself, not the entire country."

"How is it that you support yourself, dear?" Mrs. Benjamin asked.

"I rob banks," he said.

"That's a bit risky, isn't it?" Noah's mother asked.

We all stared at her. Was she kidding?

"Mother, he just said he's a bank robber!" Beth snapped. "A more appropriate answer would have been to pick up the phone and call the police."

"I was kidding," Emmett said, eyeing both mother and daughter Benjamin as though they were insane. "I'm in between jobs at the moment. But I'm working on a novel."

"It's brilliant," Charla said. "Just brilliant."

"What's it about?" Mrs. Benjamin asked.

"Existentialism," Emmett said.

"Isn't that nice," Mrs. Benjamin replied.

"Mother, you don't even know what existentialism is," Beth muttered.

Noah squeezed my hand under the table.

"Well, it sounds interesting," Mrs. Benjamin said. "I understand you just moved back to New York from—where were you living, dear?"

"Here and there," Emmett said. "I'm going to base myself in New York for a while since Charla just started school here, at NYU."

My grandmother smiled.

Charla put her hand atop Emmett's, but he pulled his hand away. "So, Eloise," she said. "Where are you in the wedding plans?"

I had a mouth full of potato salad. "Tomorrow I'm going gown shopping."

My grandmother beamed. "And I'm going along. I can't get around easily, but I wouldn't miss this for the world."

When you see the gown Astrid has in store for me, I'm sure you'll wish you had missed it. I had no doubt my gown would be made of parachute material or have wings or even an engine.

"Crazy as this sounds, I always liked the idea of getting married at City Hall," Charla said. "Just me, my love and the legal stuff."

Emmett was staring at his plate, which he'd barely touched.

"You two serious?" Noah's mother asked, wagging a finger between Emmett and Charla.

Noah shook his head. "Mom…" He smiled at Emmett and Charla. "You have to understand, she's an amateur matchmaker in her neighborhood. Marriage is all she thinks about."

"Me too," Charla responded quietly.

Aha, so Charla was serious but Emmett was his usual self. Even so, the fact that he was still dating the same woman a year later was new for Emmett. I wondered how long he'd been dating her before I met her in my doorway last year.

Emmett was studying his potato pancakes. "Uh, is there any sour cream?"

The women at the table, except myself and Beth Benjamin, flew over themselves to get the dish of sour cream to Emmett.

"Well, I think weddings are all a huge waste of money and other people's time," Beth muttered, layering smoked salmon on a bagel. "What's the divorce rate? Fifty percent?"

"Cynical!" Noah chided. "There's the fifty percent that last till death do us part. That'll be me and Eloise. Tottering around in our nineties, holding hands." We were actually holding hands at that very moment, under the table. He brought our hands onto the table in a united front to emphasize his point. "And, Beth, don't forget that your own parents have been married for thirty-four years."

"Well, I guess you got me there," she muttered.

Beth was a mutterer. I glanced at her. She was on the verge of tears.

Beth Benjamin had never endeared herself to anyone, but she was going through a divorce and it had to be pretty hard to have to sit through endless conversations about her brother's la-di-da wedding that would be featured in a national magazine.

Note to self: Invite Beth somewhere—if she says nothing snarky in the next five minutes.

She blew it in under four. "And, I wouldn't get too excited about going wedding-gown shopping with Eloise," Beth told my grandmother. "Have you seen the bridesmaids dresses we're wearing? They're Halloween costumes."

"They're *couture*," I defended.

"I think they're great," Noah said. "Very high fashion."

Score one for my fiancé. He hadn't even seen the dress.

"Well, weddings aren't about high fashion," Beth retorted. "They're about love."

"We've got plenty of that," Noah said, still holding my hand.

★ ★ ★

That night, Noah and I lay in bed, watching the *Late Show with David Letterman.* The Hilton sisters were guests.

"You really don't mind that you might be wearing a space suit on your wedding day?" I asked.

He shook his head. "As long as I lift up the veil and your face is underneath it, I don't care about anything else."

"I'm very lucky," I whispered.

"No, *I'm* lucky."

I laughed. He had no idea how much I needed that.

chapter 7

Once again, half the staff of *Wow Weddings* was squeezed into tiny It's Your Day bridal salon. Front and center were two mannequins covered by drop cloths. Astrid, wearing a wool suit so blindingly white it was difficult to look at her, stood between them, snapping her fingers to bring everyone to attention.

My grandmother squeezed my hand. "I'm so excited to see your wedding gown!"

Are you there, God? It's me, Eloise. Please let it be remotely normal.

Astrid cleared her throat. "I have chosen two gowns that I feel most reflect the tastes of today's Classic and Today's Modern Brides. I will now unveil the Classic Bride's gown—"

"Um, Astrid?" Philippa interrupted. "I don't see any other racks with our names on them."

"And?" Astrid said.

"Well, what if we prefer another wedding gown? Philippa asked. "Don't we get to choose another one? Like we did with the bridesmaid dresses?"

Astrid shook her head. "No."

"But—"

"Philippa, do you have any idea what a Princess-brand wedding gown costs? The gown I have selected with the esteemed help of Princess's marketing director and advertising director has a price point of twenty-two thousand dollars. This gown—" she swept her arms at the mannequin on her left "—is the gown that Princess wants to push as this season's must-have. Therefore, it is the gown you will choose."

Add air quotes!

Philippa looked at me. She took a deep breath. "Okay, I'm ready."

Astrid rolled her eyes. "Oh, *are* you? Let us begin then. I will now unveil Princess's silk and satin hand-beaded wedding gown, the Crown Jewel."

Under the drop cloth was my Audrey Hepburn dress.

"Oh, Eloise, isn't this gown just lovely!" my grandmother whispered. "With all Philippa's worry, I was expecting something awful!"

Philippa stared at the mannequin. "Um, Astrid?"

"What is it, Philippa?" Astrid asked, monotone.

"It's really pretty," Philippa said. "But it's not my dream dress."

"Philippa, this feature isn't about your dream. It's about advertising revenue and circulation."

"But—"

Astrid ignored her. "Where is the Classic Bride's mother or maid of honor?" she called out as she glanced around. "We'll begin shooting oohs and aahs in exactly three minutes."

No one stepped forward.

"Philippa, I don't see your mother or your maid of honor," Astrid said.

"My maid of honor is right there," Philippa replied, pointing at…

Me.

Huh?

She ran over to me and pulled me aside. "Eloise, I would be so honored if you'd be my maid of honor! After all, if it weren't for you, I wouldn't even be getting married!"

But— *We're not even really friends. And what about your gazillions of size-four girlfriends?*

"Classic Bride and the Classic Bride's maid of honor, please move to makeup for a quick touching up," Astrid instructed.

News flash for Astrid, supposed efficiency expert: It would take less breath to use our *names.*

Devlin's assistant slid a headband so tightly onto my scalp that my head hurt. She poofed my hair up around it, then handed me a Pepto-Bismol-pink cardigan to put on. Philippa was given a dusting of blush, her blond hair was pulled back in a baby blue headband, and she was tossed a baby blue cashmere tank top to change into.

A moment later, we were positioned around the mannequin wearing *my* gown.

"Philippa," Devlin snapped. "Smile like you mean it."

"But I don't mean it," she whispered to me. "I don't want to wear this boring gown."

"Just pretend for the shoot," I told her. "Remember, it's not about the dress, it's about Parker. And you love him, right?"

She nodded. "I love him like crazy."

"So pretend the gown is Parker."

She beamed, Devlin snapped.

Astrid clapped her hands. "Okay, we will now unveil the Modern Bride's gown. At a price point of twenty-six thousand dollars—"

Whoa.

"I present Rendezvous Squared's must-have gown for the season," Astrid continued before unveiling the mannequin.

No.

No.

Please let this be a dream.

"Are those feathers?" my grandmother whispered.

I was going to be Big Bird at my wedding. And unlike in my dream, I didn't want to be.

Philippa gasped. "But that's *my* gown!"

You can have it. Please.

"Philippa," Astrid droned. "We discussed this last week. As evidenced by *Wow*'s choice, this fashion-forward, twenty-six-thousand-dollar gown from Rendezvous Squared is the manifestation of modern."

No, it's what Big Bird's bride would wear for their *Sesame Street* nuptials.

"According to the major fashion houses, yellow is the new black," Mini-Astrid said.

"But no one wears a black wedding gown," I pointed out. "So if yellow is the new black, it can't be the new white also! And *that's* the color we should be going for, don't you think? The new white!"

"There is no new white, Eloise," Astrid said. "White will always be white."

So much for my using fashion doublespeak against the queen of fashion doublespeak. "I see. Thank you for the clarification."

While Philippa and I went off to a corner to hyperventilate, my grandmother was sent into the beauty and fashion editors' clutches. Five minutes later, Grams emerged wearing an "aunt of the bride" fuchsia leather jacket with a rhinestone-studded lapel and matching long skirt. She looked surprisingly good in hot pink.

"Let's shoot a roll with Eloise wearing her veil," Astrid instructed Devlin. She snapped her fingers and Mini-Astrid pushed over another mannequin whose head was covered by a drop cloth.

Astrid unveiled the naked mannequin. My veil was leather. A very thin, pale yellow leather, perforated with tiny holes that spelled out *peace* in lowercase letters.

I was all for peace. *But this is war,* I shouted mentally at Astrid, who was beaming at the Big Bird dress.

I was summoned to the beauty editor for hair flattening. The fashion editor attached the veil.

"Dynamite," Astrid said, nodding at the veil. Her minions nodded too.

"Is that leather, dear?" my grandmother asked.

I nodded.

"What does that say across the top?" she asked, squinting at the tiny holes.

It says SUCKER.

"Peace," I told her.

She chuckled. "What a funny thing to advertise for a wedding."

"Trendy magazines and their ways," I said with a shrug. If my almost eighty-year-old grandmother could have a sense of humor, so could I. Right?

Devlin ordered me and Grams into position around the Big Bird gown. "All right, Modern Bride and Modern Grandmother—smile!"

"You're so lucky, Eloise," Philippa breathed, gazing with dreamy eyes at the Modern Bride gown.

To: JaneGregg@PoshPublishing.com
From: EManfred@WowWeddings.org
Re: Help
I am in desperate need of a Flirt Night Round Table. Just wait till you see my wedding gown. Ack!

From: JaneGregg@PoshPublishing.com
To: EManfred@WowWeddings.org
Re: FNRT
How about tomorrow afternoon after our bridesmaid dress fitting? P.S. Your wedding gown can't be worse than the dress you're wearing at my wedding. Can it?

The moment I arrived at A Fancy Affair bridal salon in Forest Hills, Queens, on Saturday morning, I was greeted by Jane's aunt Ina's signature scent, Norell, a kiss on the cheek, a quick comment about the weather and an even quicker question about how my own wedding plans were going. I was then laden with dress bag and shoes and instructed to change in dressing-room two and to step onto platform three in fitting-area one.

A seamstress with a tape measure around her neck and a box of pins in her hand was waiting for me when I walked out of the dressing room. I expected her to laugh at the dress, but she didn't. She patted the third platform (there were five set up in a row in front of a wall of mirrors), kneeled down, opened her pin box and set to work.

"Are you Miss America?"

The seamstress speaks! During the past ten minutes, she hadn't said a word other than "Turn to the left. No, the other left."

I glanced down at the seamstress. She had two sharp pins in her mouth. Could you talk around pins?

"*Are* you Miss America?"

Ah. A mini-ventriloquist emerged. Behind the seamstress hid a little girl, absolutely adorable and six or seven years old, shyly peeking up at me. She was decked out in a flower girl's ensemble, frilly yellow dress, shiny Mary Janes and daisy halo.

"Just for today and again when it's ready for fitting number two and then again on the Fourth of July," I told her with a wink.

Her mouth dropped open, and she ran out of the fitting room yelling, "Mommy, Mommy, Miss America's in there!"

"What would Miss America be doing in Queens?" a woman's voice asked in the next fitting room.

"She makes lots of personal appearances," another voice said.

Yes, fellow Americans, it is true. My beauty, my bright-white smile, my president's wife's wave, my dream for us all—insert dramatic heartfelt glance at the audience—to just get along, have won me the crown! Yet here I am, in my best friend Jane's hometown of Forest Hills, Queens, a schlep on the subway from my Manhattan neighborhood—

A few heads poked in and eyed me up and down. Miss America must not get a lot a lot of privacy. "Sweetie," said one of them, "that's not Miss America. That's just a bridesmaid."

I beg your pardon. I was a *maid of honor.* My dress had a row of extra stars along the neckline to prove it.

"But why is she wearing a red, white and blue dress with stars all over it if she's not Miss America?" the girl asked.

It was a very good question.

They all stared at me.

"July Fourth wedding," I explained.

"How patriotic," said one of the head pokers.

I had a better word to describe the dress, but as Jane, her aunt Ina and her cousin Dana had just walked in, I decided to keep my adjectives to myself.

"Eloise! Don't you look lovely!" Jane's aunt, Ina Dreer, said. She beamed at my reflection in the mirror, her hand over her heart. "Oh, my! Girls, doesn't she look beautiful? What did I tell you? Was I right or what?"

Or what, Jane mouthed at me.

"Where are Amanda and Natasha?" Ina asked, glancing at her watch. "They're seven minutes late."

"Aunt Ina, they're coming from Manhattan," Jane pointed out. "Give them a break."

"Well *I* came from Chappaqua," Dana said, brushing snow off her Ugg boots. "And I managed to get here on time. And Eloise came from Manhattan, and she got here *early.*"

"Amanda and Natasha and I came together," I said. "They stopped in the Starbucks on the corner. They had cravings for peppermint mochas."

As Ina and Dana stared at their watches and muttered that we *all* wanted a cup of coffee and the nerve of some people, Jane hopped up on the platform next to mine.

"So am I right?" Jane asked. "Or could your gown really be worse than this?"

I smiled at her in the mirror. "Now that I'm wearing it, I'm actually not sure. I've definitely never felt so American."

She laughed. "Is your gown really that bad?"

"Not if you like yellow sequins and feathers—lots of them."

She smiled and slung an arm around me. "Well, it can't be worse than the polka-dot bows on Amanda's bridesmaid dresses."

Actually, it was a million times worse.

"Sorry we're late!" Amanda and Natasha chimed in unison as they rushed in, a light dusting of snow on their hair. Amanda was gulping a venti Starbucks coffee and shaking snow off her long blond ponytail, and Natasha was rocking Summer's stroller back and forth. "Caffeine run."

Ina waved her hands dismissively and ran over to the baby stroller. "Let me see that sweet baby! Oh, she's sleeping. She's so beautiful!"

As everyone ran to the stroller to get a peek at Summer, I tried to step down from my platform, but the seamstress grabbed my ankle. "Do not move, please!" she barked.

Yes, ma'am!

"Summer, Auntie Eloise says hello," I whispered.

"Okay, let's not dawdle in here," Ina commanded, handing dress bags to Amanda and Natasha. "Hurry into a dressing room and change, and then come back in here immediately. Natasha, dear, you'll have to wake up the baby so that we can try on her dress," Ina added, pint-size dress bag over her arm.

Natasha raised an eyebrow. "You actually want to wake a sleeping two-year-old? Do you prize peace and quiet?"

Ina sighed. "I suppose we can wait until the very end. Okay, girls, shoo! Change!" She rushed out, shouting, "Seamstresses, we're ready for three more in fitting area one. Jane, here's your gown. Go try it on."

Bossy! Jane mouthed when Ina was busy eagle-eyeing the seamstress's work on my hem.

Amanda, Natasha and Dana came out of the dressing

rooms in their patriotic chic and stepped up on wooden platforms.

The three of them were so pretty, they'd make the Big Bird gown look good. Natasha was a dead ringer for Nicole Kidman, even mistaken for her sometimes. Amanda was tiny, with long blond hair and huge blue eyes that she now hid behind severe eyeglasses to be taken more seriously at the law firm where she worked as a paralegal. And Jane's cousin Dana, also tiny and also blond, was very attractive, which you realized only when she wasn't talking.

"Omigod!" Dana squealed as she stepped up on her platform. "I *love* this dress!" She turned to the left and to the right, admiring her petite figure and playing with her wispy blond bangs.

We all stared at her. Was she kidding? Did Dana Dreer Fishkill have a sense of humor, after all?

No, she was serious. She was preening. She started singing "Living In America" (she was no James Brown) and almost fell off her platform.

"Well, at least it's not rubber," Amanda said, winking at me. "But it's also not free."

"Oh, Dana!" Ina gushed at her daughter. "You look so beautiful! How did I get so lucky? First my baby gets married to a wonderful, wealthy man, and now my Jane, my beloved niece, my late sister's only child, is getting married. And it's all my doing!"

It sort of was. Ina had been trying to fix up Jane with the guy who lived next door to Jane's grandmother, but Jane figured him for a nerd, said no thanks and dated half of Manhattan to find a date for Dana's wedding. Then she met the next-door neighbor—Ethan—at Dana's wedding, and it was love at first sight.

"Love is so great," Dana squealed. "When Jane was getting fitted for my wedding, she wasn't seeing anyone. In fact, she even made up having a boyfriend to take to my wedding. Do you remember that, Jane? All that trouble you went through, trying to find Mr. Right, when my mom had the perfect guy for you all along. If only you'd listened to Mom, you'd have saved yourself a lot of trouble."

"I like trouble," Jane shouted from behind the dressing-room curtain.

Dana shook her butt as she sang an off-key version of the chorus of Bruce Springsteen's "Born in the USA." "Larry is going to love me in this dress. I can't wait to try it on for him. Ooh, I'd better not. He'll rip it right off me!"

Ina wagged a finger at her daughter. "Dana Dreer Fishkill, don't you dare get pregnant until July *fifth!* No matter how badly I want a grandbaby, you have to fit into that dress come the Fourth of July!" She laughed. "That goes for all of you girls. No getting pregnant until *after* Jane's wedding."

Pregnant? Could you get pregnant if your boyfriend was always away on business?

"No losing or gaining an ounce, for that matter," Ina added.

"Aunt Ina, stop torturing my bridesmaids," Jane called from her dressing room. "Okay, I'm coming in. Ready or not…"

As Jane walked in the room, all of our hands flew to our mouths. I immediately started to cry. Ina grabbed Jane in a tight hug.

This was a wedding gown.

"You look so beautiful!" Ina said, tears in her eyes. "Oh, would your mother be proud, Jane. If she could see you now… Oh, Jane."

I wondered what my mother would think of me in the Big Bird gown. She had always liked the color yellow.

Jane's gown was exquisite. Strapless, with a white ribbon across the empire waist, the white satin flowed to the floor. Her veil was long, and she wore elbow-length white gloves. There wasn't a hint of red, white or blue anywhere.

But guess what colors her bridal bouquet would be?

"Look what I found at the drugstore when I was buying panty hose on sale," Ina said, twirling a cheap silver garter around her index finger. "I'll bet I can find red, white and blue garters for the Fourth of July!"

Jane, Amanda, Natasha and I shared a look of horror.

"The good news is that not one of you will be forced to line up to catch the bouquet at the wedding," Jane said. "We're all taken women! I'm including boyfriended Natasha."

"Whew!" Natasha said with a wink.

"I don't see why single women have such a problem with the bouquet toss," Dana said, practicing her cousin-of-the-bride smile in the mirror. "I mean, if you catch it, you're next!"

"Not every single woman is obsessed with marriage," I pointed out.

"You're one to talk," Dana said. "You're getting a free dream wedding from a major magazine. It'll be like the entire world is coming to your wedding!"

"For three dollars and ninety-five cents," Amanda said, citing the cover price of *Wow Weddings.*

Dana ignored her. "So, Janey, who's going to walk you down the aisle?"

Ina gave her daughter one of her famous sharp glances.

"I just mean that she can borrow Daddy or Larry," Dana defended herself.

"What do *you* want?" Ina asked Jane. "This is about you, after all. It's your day."

Jane almost laughed.

"What's so funny?" Ina asked.

"Nothing, Aunt Ina," Jane said. "Actually, I've given the question of who's going to walk me down the aisle some thought. I want Eloise, Amanda, Dana and Natasha to give me away."

Ina was horrified. "But, honey, that's hardly normal! Friends giving away the bride?"

"It's right in keeping with the Independence Day theme," Jane pointed out. "My gal pals delivering me from single life to married life."

"I suppose," Ina said. "Well, if it's what you want. But it's hardly traditional."

Jane nodded and smiled at us. "It's what I want."

If a father walking his daughter down the aisle was traditional, I could absolutely cross it off my list of Things To Worry About.

Flirt Night Round Table Discussion 1,000,001: Eloise is wearing a Big Bird gown to marry a guy she's having heart palpitations about marrying.

"Not heart palpitations," Jane said. "Heart*burn*. Self-inflicted heartburn. Caused by transferring anxiety about one thing to another that doesn't deserve it."

"Are you a book editor or a headshrinker?" I asked.

"I'm your best friend" was her answer.

"I think the heartburn is from this salsa," Amanda said. "It's way too spicy for me."

We were in a Mexican restaurant around the corner

from A Fancy Affair, toasting our freedom from the bouquet toss and sharing a huge plate of chicken nachos. Summer was crumbling tortilla chips onto the floor.

"And, anyway, who cares about the gown?" Amanda said. "It's the guy that counts. And Noah is great."

He was. He definitely was.

Jane eyed me. "Okay, Eloise, I see from your expression that there's a *but* coming. Let's have it."

"I look awful in yellow," I said.

Consensus: The Big Bird gown is going to be taken off your body seven hours later by your hot new husband who you *do* want to marry, so who cares about a few feathers? And haven't you heard, yellow is the new black?

I felt much better.

Until Amanda mentioned that my lingerie would probably have feathers too.

Dear Wedding Diary,

   My favorite character from Sesame Street has always been Elmo, not Big Bird.

Wow Weddings Memorandum

To: Eloise Manfred
From: Astrid O'Connor
Re: Wedding-Planning Diary Entry #2
Eloise,
I'm afraid I don't understand your references to Big Bird and Elmo. And if I don't understand these references, American women will not understand these references. I've asked Maura to draft the entry for you as an example for future entries. Please do your best to emulate her style and word count. —AO

★ ★ ★

Oops. I'd actually spent an hour writing a ridiculous account of how yellow was the new black for the Modern Bride and how very Sarah Jessica Parker I felt twirling around in the gown. But, by accident, I must have given Astrid the diary entry I wrote for my own sanity.

It was my first smile of the day.

chapter 8

For the past few weeks, the reception area of *Wow Weddings* magazine had turned into the hottest ticket in town for the wedding industry. From 9:00 a.m. to 5:00 p.m., the three-seater leather sofa and four upholstered chairs were filled by advertisers hopeful of getting their wedding wares past Astrid O'Connor. Entrepreneurs laden with samples of everything from hosiery to bouquets to hair combs. Caterers and photographers and travel agencies and jewelry shops.

This morning, every seat and square inch were taken by men and children. As I pulled open the glass double doors, a gob of what looked like red Play-Doh hit me in the stomach.

"Gotcha!" announced a three-year-old boy, who then went running down the hall, gleefully shrieking and tipping over wastepaper baskets in his wake.

"Bradford, you come back here this instant!" shouted

an attractive man in a suit splattered with stains. He chased the child around a corner.

Suddenly a baby wailed.

Was I in a playground? A nursery school? What was going—

Ah. Today was Father/Grooms-To-Be day. Today's Brides weren't enough for Astrid for the all-important June issue. Her latest brainstorm was to capitalize on Father's Day, as well. Her plan was to feature four grooms-to-be who were also fathers and one groom-*and*-father-to-be.

The four dads, ranging from Wall Street businessman to East Village grunge, and three children, ranging from a baby in a car seat to the Play-Doh-throwing toddler, who was now tearing pages out of a pile of *Wow Weddings* magazines on the coffee table, to a sullen teenager, plus a very pregnant woman, were squeezed into the small space.

The receptionist, trying to tempt the toddler with a stuffed bride doll left over from another promotion, looked as if she was going to cry. "No, don't touch that," Lorna said to the boy, who grabbed her appointment book and was shaking it.

"Daddy, do I have an agent?" the teenage girl asked, twirling her long, brown hair around her finger. "My friend says you need an agent to be a model."

"Honey, this isn't really modeling," the father said. "We're going to be in an article about fathers who are getting married."

"So what am I doing here?" the girl said.

The man turned to the East Village guy. "Hey, buddy, maybe your baby's crying because she needs a diaper change. I can't hear myself think over that wailing."

"I don't believe in diapers," East Village Dad said. "My wife and I are into natural expellment."

We all stared at him.

"Duh, kidding," he said, rolling his eyes.

"Jesus, can't you do something about that baby's wailing!" barked the toddler's dad. "He's driving my kid batty!"

"Too bad!" East Village Dad snapped. "And it's no wonder she's crying. She's being sold out at two months as a child star. A pawn for the greedy! I got talked into allowing this, but I won't stand for it!" He stood up and wheeled the carriage out of the room.

And then there were three. And blessed quiet.

Five minutes later, I was summoned into Astrid's office.

She sat behind her huge desk, tapping a beige talon against her cheek. "The most outrageous idea occurred to me," she said. "We need to find a young, hip male model to replace the young father who left. Would your brother be interested in filling in? He fits the bill. We'd supply the baby, of course."

Unbelievable. But this was how Emmett's life worked. Offers—and babies—came to *him*.

I stopped by Charla's apartment after work, curious about where Emmett was living. Turned out she had a very nice studio apartment in a doorman building near NYU, where I myself had gone to college.

"Graduate-school housing," she explained when I arrived. Emmett was sprawled on her futon, reading *Ulysses* and popping red grapes into his mouth. "I'm not being subsidized by my parents or anything."

"I wouldn't think less of you if you were," I assured her.

"A lot of people do," she said. "You have to be really careful to come off as poor as possible around some people."

"Well, speaking of money," I said, and explained to her and Emmett about Astrid's offer.

Emmett threw *Ulysses* at the wall. "They want me to be some baby's fake father for idiot photographs in a magazine? Are they fucking kidding me?"

"Emmett, sweetie," Charla said, "it's five hundred bucks! We could—" she coughed à la Mrs. Benjamin "—*really* use the money right now."

He let out a breath and sank down on the sofa, then bent his head to his knees, his face in his hands.

"I'm pregnant," Charla explained.

Oh.

"I need some air," Emmett muttered. He grabbed his book, the stalk of grapes and his jacket and practically ran out of the apartment.

"I could use some air too," Charla said to me. "Wanna go for a walk?"

We headed up Broadway. Charla stopped at a street vendor to buy new gloves, since one of hers had a hole in the palm. She chose a pink chenille pair with little pompoms on the knuckles.

"Let me get them for you," I offered. "Pregnancy gift."

She smiled. "It's okay. I can afford it. I have a really great student loan and a part-time job at the Gap, so I can get a good discount on clothes, maternity clothes and baby clothes."

I nodded. "That's good."

She rubbed her hands together. Her little pompoms shook. "It's so cold out. Are you hungry? We could grab some dinner."

Charla had a craving for beef tacos, so we found an inexpensive Mexican restaurant a couple of blocks away. Despite the fact that I wasn't hungry, I ordered a chicken burrito to make the minimum for sitting at a table.

She poured three containers of hot salsa on her taco.

"I'm pregnant," she repeated, letting out a deep breath. "I can't quite believe it."

"How far along are you?"

"Just eight weeks. I know you're not supposed to tell anyone until you're twelve weeks to be safe, but I couldn't *not* tell Emmett, and then, well, it just sort of came out before at the apartment."

"So Emmett was a little freaked, huh?" I asked, having no doubt what his reaction had been.

She nodded, her pretty, green eyes filling with tears. "He was blown away." She sniffled. "I'm still so hungry. I'm going up to order another taco. Do you want something?"

I shook my head and watched her walk up to the counter. She was pregnant with my brother's child. My niece. My nephew. A new Manfred.

I was blown away.

Charla came back with two more tacos. She inhaled one, then downed a Snapple iced tea. "He didn't say a word for, like, ten minutes after I told him. And then he asked if I saw my doctor and if everything was okay and I told him it was and he asked me if I wanted to have the baby and I said yes, and he nodded and he hasn't mentioned it since."

"Which was when?" I asked.

"Four days ago," she said, biting into her third taco.

The baby would be gorgeous. Between Charla's delicate blond beauty and Emmett's "you could be a model" great looks, little Manfred was going to be a Summer.

"How long have you known Emmett?" I asked.

"We've been dating almost four years on and off."

I almost spit out my mouthful of Corona. "*Four years?* You've been dating Emmett for *four* years?"

How could Emmett have been dating Charla for four

years? Why hadn't he ever introduced her to the family? Brought her to a family holiday? Mentioned her name, for that matter! Sigh. I really *didn't* know Emmett at all—and he clearly wanted it that way.

Charla nodded. "Four in March. Well, February, really. We met on leap year, isn't that funny? This is the first year we'll be celebrating on the actual day we met."

I laughed. "We have something in common. I'm getting married on February 29."

"You're kidding!" she said. "That's so crazy."

"No, it's so *modern,*" I corrected, filling her in a bit about Astrid O'Connor and her vision of a Modern Bride. "Noah told me there was no such thing as a free wedding, but I didn't listen. Now it's too late."

Her eyes filled with tears. "Emmett told me he'd never commit to me but I wouldn't listen. And now I'm pregnant with his baby." Tears rolled down her cheeks.

I scooted my chair over to her side of the table. "Charla, four years is a long time. And you're still together. He might not realize it, but he clearly *is* committed."

"You think so?" she asked. "Even though he takes off for months at a time? The only reason he came back last week was because he wanted to see some band playing at the Beacon."

"Or so he said," I told her. "I'm sure he came back because he missed you."

Suddenly I wondered if he came back for *me*. Because I called. I'd assumed he was in New York already or that my need coincided with his plans.

Charla shrugged and crunched on a tortilla chip.

"And when you met," I added, "he was only, what, twenty-four? He's twenty-nine now. And there's a baby on the way. Maybe he'll surprise you, Charla."

"You think so?" she asked again.

Actually, I had no idea.

"Because I'm ninety-nine percent sure he'll leave," she continued, "when it really sinks in. Right now he's turning it around in his mind, trying to see a way out, but there isn't any. If he wants to be with me, he gets a baby."

"*His* baby," I pointed out.

"*His* baby, *a* baby," she said. "It doesn't make a difference to him."

How could it not?

"I'm sure he'll be gone by my first ultrasound appointment. This isn't what he's about."

I shook my head. "Unbelievable. How is someone allowed not to be about *responsibility?*"

She shrugged. "It's not what he wants right now."

Emmett, Emmett, Emmett. How did you turn into a carbon copy of the man you last saw at age two?

I slammed my palm down on the table. "Self-absorbed, selfish jerk!"

She smiled through a sniffle. "Hey, you're talking about the father of my baby."

We both smiled weak smiles and bundled back into our coats and gloves and hats. "Did you tell your parents?" I asked as we headed outside.

"There's just my mom," she said. "And she told me I was a fool if I had the baby. That I finally found what I wanted to do with my life, got myself in grad school after years of temping and now I was going to have a kid with a guy who didn't even have health insurance or know what a 401K Plan was."

"What do you think?" I asked.

She touched her belly. "I think I'm going to have a baby. Make that I *know* I'm going to have a baby. I might be exhausted and I might have to find help where I can, but I know I can do it. That's really three-quarters of success— *knowing* you can do it."

I was impressed by her attitude. "Then a success you will be." I put my arm around her shoulder. "And besides, you've got me now—and I take my auntly duties *very* seriously."

She stopped and looked at me and hugged me for a long time right in the middle of Broadway.

chapter 9

The next morning, another father was causing a commotion of his own in the hallway at *Wow Weddings*.

"Who's the boss around here?" Philippa's dad bellowed, his gold watch gleaming in the early-morning sunlight shining through the window. "I want to speak to the boss right away!"

"Daddy!" Philippa squealed, trying to pull him into her cubicle. "Stop—you're embarrassing me in front of all my colleagues!"

Astrid's assistant, Carol, came running to Philippa's cubicle. "Is something wrong, Mr. Wills?"

"You bet there is, little lady," he said. "I want to know why my precious baby girl is stuck working in a cubicle when she should have a corner office!"

Carol's eyes widened.

"Daddy!" Philippa yelled again, but she was fighting a smile.

"I'm just joshing around!" Mr. Wills said, slapping his thigh and throwing back his head.

Philippa swatted her father's shoulder. "Daddy, you're embarrassing me!"

But it wasn't embarrassing. It was...nice. There was nothing not nice about a father loving his daughter. For the past fifteen minutes, Philippa's father had been hanging on her every word, looking at every article she'd ever proofread and calling her his precious baby girl at least ten times per minute.

Mr. Wills wagged a finger at me. "Before I left my office, my secretary chased after me with her huge appointment book and a worried expression and said, 'Mr. Wills, you can't leave right now—you have a shareholders' meeting in half an hour!' Do you want to know what I said?"

We were all waiting on pins and needles!

He pointed a finger at me. "I looked her right in the eye and said, 'Mary, my baby girl comes first.'"

"Oh, Daddy!" Philippa said, flying into his arms.

Okay, *now* it was getting embarrassing.

"Eleanor, is it?" he said, glancing at me.

"Eloise," I corrected.

"Eloise. Like that little cartoon girl in Paris."

I smiled. "Actually, the Plaza."

He looked at me quizzically. "Well, I'll tell you, Eleanor, I'm not surprised Philippa is working for a big-deal national magazine. Words were always her thing. She won the statewide spelling bee two years in a row."

When, in preschool? Philippa couldn't even spell *officiant*. She asked me how to spell it this morning when we were filling out forms for who would be performing our ceremonies. Apparently, clergy persons and judges didn't offer free services in exchange for ads in *Wow Weddings*.

"And look at her now, all grown up and getting married," her father went on. He started to break down, honest to goodness, then said, "Ignore me. I'm just all choked up."

I could hear Astrid's heels clicking toward us. Her perfume preceded her as she rounded the corner, Devlin a step behind her.

"Devlin, let's get some candids of Daddy crying tears of joy that his baby is all grown up," Astrid said.

Devlin did his usual snapping at his assistant, who set up the lighting, and then he directed Daddy and Philippa to produce a few fake tears.

"That's perfect, Dad," Devlin said.

Click. Click. Click-click.

"I am so proud of you, baby girl," Mr. Wills told Philippa as he pinched her cheek. "I cannot wait to walk you down the aisle."

"I love you, Daddy," Philippa said.

Hug. Kiss.

"Philippa," Astrid said. "I couldn't be more pleased with how well your shoots are going. This one in particular—candids in your office environment, the classic girl at work, helping her country, helping the economy until her wedding day when she can concentrate on philanthropic pursuits, both grand scale and grassroots, and babies, of course, at least three—is really going to strike a chord with the American reader."

I wondered if Astrid was normal at home. In her relationships with her husband and family and friends. Could you be a completely different person at work than you were outside of work? Probably not. Her husband had to be a trip himself.

"Um, Astrid," Philippa said. "I'm not expected to quit when I return from my honeymoon, am I?"

"Of course not, Philippa," Astrid replied. "You'll resign beforehand, so that we can deduct those two weeks from your vacation pay."

Dead silence, except for the sound of Philippa swallowing.

Astrid rolled her eyes. "It was a joke, people. Honestly, does anyone have a sense of humor around here?"

"She must have had sex last night," I whispered to Philippa.

"Eloise, I do hope you were paying attention to the spirit of these shots," Astrid said. "Especially with the deceased-mother angle, your Father of the Modern Bride shots are going to be more touching than they even need to be. After all, the Modern Bride is also Daddy's Little Girl."

"That is so true, Astrid," Philippa agreed, hugging her father.

"By the way, Eloise," Astrid said. "I moved up your Father of the Modern Bride shoot to next Monday. Please memo me if that's a problem."

Hey, Astrid, here's a memo: It's a problem.

Delayed reactions were interesting. One minute you could be peeling potatoes in your kitchen for homemade French fries as a surprise for your fiancé, who was an addict, and the next, you could be crying your eyes out.

"Eloise? What's wrong?" Noah asked from the kitchen doorway.

"Nothing," I said. "Just the onions."

"But you're not chopping onions."

"Oh."

He peered at me. "Eloise?"

"What if you're not back in time for ring shopping on

Monday afternoon?" I asked, tears rolling down my cheeks. "Fiancés are supposed to be there."

"I'll be there," he said. "Two o'clock. Round Rings, West Broadway."

"But what if you can't?" I said.

"Eloise, there is no *can't*. I'll be there no matter what."

"This potato peeler is no good!" I shrieked. "It doesn't peel right."

"Eloise, honey, what is wrong? Talk to me."

I closed my eyes. "I have a father."

He took the peeler out of my hand and set it down. My hands fell to my sides.

"I have a father," I said again, tears falling down my cheeks.

Noah took me by the hand and led me into the living room. I sat on the sofa and stared at my shoes.

"I've been pretending I don't have a father since I was five, but I have one," I said. "The reason he's not walking me down the aisle at my wedding isn't because he's dead or in Switzerland on business."

Noah held me for a few minutes. He didn't say anything and neither did I.

"I really wanted to make you those fries to eat in the cab on the way to the airport," I told him between sniffles. "But you're already gonna be late as it is."

"I'm not going, El," he said. "I'm staying right here."

"But…"

But don't make me expect this. Don't do things like this that I really need, because I might start needing them.

I burst into tears.

"Tell me about your father, Eloise. You never talk about him. The times I've asked, you've made a joke and changed the subject and I haven't pressed you. Tell me."

I shook my head. "I can't."

"Sweetheart, it's okay."

"But it's not okay!" I yelled. "It's not okay to just leave your children! It's not okay for them to grow up thinking their own father doesn't love them. It's not okay! He's not dead, like my mother. He *chose* to leave. It's not okay!"

I sobbed in Noah's arms for another five minutes. Huge wracking sobs that hadn't come out of me since my mother died.

"No, Eloise, it's not okay. What is okay is for you to open up to me, to tell me things. Things that are important, like this."

"But—"

He lifted my chin. "No buts, Eloise. We're getting married. Husband and wife. Team."

"But it doesn't mean anything," I said. "Husband and wife, father and daughter—they're just *words.* They don't mean anything."

"The words themselves might not mean anything, Eloise, but the *people* do. It's about the *people.* It's about you and me."

I don't know. I don't know. I don't know.

"Tell me about your father, Eloise. Tell me what happened."

I leaned back against the sofa and stared up at the ceiling. What was there to tell Noah? That my father left because he couldn't stand the smell of French toast?

For a long time, that was what I thought. A few months after he was gone, when my mother and Emmett and I were in a diner, someone at the next table ordered French toast and I flipped out. I screamed and shook my fists and cried, according to my mother, for a half hour. I'd been inconsolable. Poor Emmett, having no idea why his sister was having the kind of tantrum he threw on a daily two-year-old basis, eyed me and stole fries off my plate.

"When you're ready, Eloise," Noah said, holding my hand. "We've got all night."

I took a deep breath and began telling Noah what I knew, which wasn't much. That my father left the day before my fifth birthday. My mother had been making French toast, my favorite food, which I wanted for breakfast, lunch, dinner and snacks (hey, I was five), but she ran out of bread. My father hated the smell of margarine sizzling in a pan and of eggy bread, so he told my mother he needed some fresh air and that he'd pick up more bread in the supermarket on the corner.

There'd been three slices of bread left. My mother gave two slices of French toast to me and one to Emmett. I kept asking for more, whining, "When's Daddy coming back?" and after a few hours, my mother gave us each a chocolate bar and disappeared into her bedroom for a little while.

Maybe a half hour later, she came back out and said that we were going to go get the bread ourselves. I told her I wasn't hungry anymore anyway, but she said we'd need bread for tomorrow, so we might as well go get it now. And so we did. I looked for my father up and down Lexington Avenue and in the supermarket, in the frozen-food aisle (he liked ice cream), in the cookie aisle, but I didn't see him. My mother, brother and I went back home, and the next morning, my mother made me as much French toast as I wanted. She put a birthday candle in the stack for me to blow out, and she formed Emmett's portion into a smiley face (he wouldn't eat anything unless she did).

I couldn't remember wondering where my father was on my birthday. I must have asked and the answer must have seemed normal to me. Probably: *Your father's work-ing. He told me to wish you a happy birthday.*

The day after that, my mother sat me on the chair by the window where she always read me a bedtime story and explained that this time, my father wasn't coming home. He'd left a short note for her where his duffel bag—always packed and at the ready for him to leave at a moment's notice—usually sat on the shelf in his closet.

The note said: *I won't be coming back. Tell Eloise and Emmett I'm sorry when they're ready to hear it.*

We were never ready to hear it.

According to my mother, my father had always said he wasn't the marrying kind (he never did marry my mother). He always said he wasn't the family kind, the sticking-around-kind. "Your father loves you and always will, but you may never see him again," she'd told me.

And I never did. The phrase *You may never see your father again,* when your father wasn't dying, was a strange concept to grasp. Because I was five, I accepted it the way you accept it when your best friend moves away. *You may never see Suzy Rothberg again* was a perfectly reasonable thing to say when she moved to California.

I was also used to him being gone. For months at a time. But he always came home, bearing nothing but himself, but he came home. There were hugs and hair ruffles, and life was fine. He'd go, he'd come back, he'd go, he'd come back. That was just the way it was. But that year, the year I turned five, the way it was changed.

We never did see Theo Manfred again—or hear from him again, not a phone call, not a birthday card. Nothing. It wasn't the kind of thing you understood when you were five or fifteen or even thirty-two.

I didn't remember much. I didn't remember waiting

for him to come home or not waiting. And Emmett remembered absolutely nothing of Theo Manfred. He only knew, as a fact, that his father left when he was two and never came back. As we were growing up, when fathers were either called for or mentioned or appeared on television, my mother would ask us if we would like to talk about our father. "No!" we would both snap in unison.

"Did you or Emmett ever try to find your father?" Noah asked.

Emmett tried once when he was sixteen. Our mother had very recently died, and Emmett and I moved into our grandmother's apartment just a few blocks away from our own. Emmett was a junior in high school and I was a freshman at NYU. He tried to find our father through Internet searches.

"I want to tell that son of a bitch that our mother is dead and now we have no parents because of him," Emmett had screamed more than once.

There were two cold addresses in upstate New York, then the trail ended, and Emmett, one angry teenager, vowed never to think about that "bastard loser" again. He never mentioned our father after that, and I didn't either.

Noah let out a deep breath. "Oh, Eloise, I'm so sorry," he said, pulling me into a hug. "That's a lot for two kids to go through. One loss, let alone two."

I took a deep breath. "I'm glad I told you."

"Me too."

"I'm glad you're here, Noah," I said.

He smiled. "Me too."

"What am I going to do? I'm a mess."

"What do you want to do?"

"I want to ask my father why he never came back. I

want to ask him why—no, *how*—he abandoned his children."

"Then do that."

I shook my head. "Even if I could work up the guts, I wouldn't know where to start looking."

He squeezed my hand. "You're not marrying an investigative journalist for nothing."

Theodore Manfred wasn't the most common name, but there were twenty-six Theodore Manfreds in the United States of America. That hadn't taken an investigative journalist; it had taken a simple search on the Internet. I was glad there were so many. If there had been just one, one Theodore Manfred in, say, Queens or Westchester, I might have spontaneously combusted.

I knew his middle name was Leo. There were four Theodore L. Manfreds. They were scattered. Ohio. Nevada. West Virginia. Pennsylvania.

Noah handed me the phone.

"Who am I calling?" I asked him. "Information in each state?"

"Your grandmother."

"My grandmother?" I repeated.

"She has to know something about your father," Noah said. "Where he's from, anything that might help narrow the search."

"But I can't ask her," I said.

"Why?"

"It's complicated."

"Try me," Noah said.

I shrugged.

"You think she'll be angry at you?"

I nodded.

...ink she'll feel it's a betrayal of your mother?"

...ded again.

...ise, I understand that, I really do," Noah said. "But ...might be wrong about how your grandmother ...s."

"But she never talks about my father. She never has."

"Probably because he doesn't come up in everyday conversation," he said. "He's not here. There's nothing to reference."

"You don't think she'll be upset that I want to find him?" I asked.

"Sweetheart, there's only one way to find out. And if she is upset, you'll get through it together."

Hi, Grams. You're my only relative in the world aside from Emmett. You won't be mad if I go searching for the man who abandoned your daughter and grandchildren without a backward glance or a penny of child support.

Will you?

My grandmother wrapped me in a tight hug. "Sweetheart, of course I'm not mad. I always knew this day would come."

"You did?"

"Come, sit," she said, stuffing a freshly baked chocolate chip cookie into my mouth and patting a chair at her kitchen table. "I'll tell you anything you want to know, Eloise. But I'm afraid there isn't much to tell."

I picked up my coffee cup. My fingers were trembling.

"Are you sure?" she asked, looking closely at me. "Are you sure you want to go down this road? If it's going to upset you this much, maybe it's not worth it. You're getting married—you should be celebrating with that hand-

some fiancé of yours, not getting all upset over so. [ ]
you had and have no control over."

"I'm sort of sure," I said.

"Then you're right to be asking questions."

I showed her the printout of Manfreds. "He could be any of these or none," I said. "I suppose I could call each number."

Uh, hello, are you the Theodore Manfred who once had two children named Eloise and Emmett?

Theodore Manfred Possibility #1: "No, sorry."

Theodore Manfred Possibility #2: "No, sorry."

Theodore Manfred Possibility #3: "No, sorry."

Theodore Manfred Possibility #4: "Yes, that's me."

Drop phone from trembling hand. Shake. Pick up phone and find voice. "Uh, well, this is your long-lost daughter, Eloise, and I was wondering why you left without a backward glance or even a penny of child support."

Silence. "Well, let's see. It was so long ago, and that's not such an easy question to answer. Nice to hear from you, though."

I wasn't so sure about that last bit. I had no idea if Theo Manfred would be happy to hear from me or not. If he would, wouldn't he have tracked me down over the years?

"You know, Eloise, when people do things they feel very uncomfortable about, they tend to rationalize so that they can live with their actions," my grandmother said. "Your father might have figured he'd come find you when you turned eighteen and try to explain why he left, and maybe that made it easier for him to stay gone. And maybe he kept moving the mark—to when you turned twenty-one, to when he got a job, to when he got over the flu. And suddenly, twenty-seven years went by."

"Is that what you think happened?" I asked. "He always meant to come back but just never could-slash-would?"

...odded. "There is no doubt in my mind that your . loved you and loved Emmett."

But how do you leave two children you love and .ever come back?" I asked. "How do you do that?" Tears, big fat wet tears, rolled down my cheeks.

"I don't know, honey," my grandmother said, patting my hand. "But I do know it wasn't about you or Emmett—or your mother. Your father just couldn't handle commitment and responsibility."

"Like Emmett," I said without thinking. I had promised my brother not to tell Grams about Charla's pregnancy.

She hesitated, but then she nodded. "Like Emmett. But I think this girlfriend of his is special. I think she may be the one to start changing the way Emmett's mind works, the way he thinks. I sense something special between them."

"If Mom couldn't change the way Theo Manfred's mind worked, then no one could," I said. "Mom was so beautiful and smart and kind and amazing."

Grams put her arm around my shoulder and squeezed. "You're absolutely right, sweetie. Which is why I'd bet my bottom dollar that your father never married, never had more children and is to this day very much alone."

"I wish I had an appetite for these cookies," I said. "They smell so good. He liked cookies, I remember that. I don't remember much, but I do remember him liking cookies. Oreos."

My grandmother nodded. "He did like sweets."

Tears came again from nowhere, and I wiped them away. "I'm such a crybaby. It's so embarrassing. Crying over someone I haven't seen since I was five."

"It's a very emotional issue, Eloise," Grams said. "You

have every right to cry. Every right to feel bad. And every right to find your father and demand your answers, if that's what you decide to do."

"I don't even know where to look," I said. "He could be anywhere."

"Well, these four states are a start," she said, scanning the addresses. "Pennsylvania. Yes—he did say he was from Pennsylvania. His parents died when he was young, a car accident, and he was raised by a grandmother."

"Did I ever meet his grandmother, my great-grandmother?"

Grams shook her head. "She'd already passed before you were born."

"I'm ready," I said. "Tell me everything there is."

"There isn't much, Eloise, but I'll tell you everything I remember."

For the next hour, she told me about a tall, good-looking man named Theodore Leo Manfred whom my mother met in a creative-writing class at the New School. He was working on a novel. He temped, he waited tables. He'd save up some money, rent a cabin in the woods in the Catskills or Pennsylvania and write for months at a time. When she became pregnant accidentally, he skedaddled.

"Did he come home when I was born?" I asked.

My grandmother hesitated, then shook her head. "You were four months old when he came back. He stayed for a few months, then went back to the cabin to write."

"Did his masterpiece at least get published?"

She shook her head. "He sent it out, but it got rejected. A number of times. He'd get very down about it and leave again."

"Why did she have another baby with him?" I shouted.

"Why would she bring another baby into this world with a father like that?"

"Don't judge your mother, Eloise," Grams scolded gently.

"Sorry."

But suddenly I knew why. There was only my mother, me and my grandmother, that was it. My mother wanted me to have someone else.

"She had Emmett so I wouldn't be alone," I said quietly.

"She had Emmett because she loved children and wanted another baby very much and was a very good mother," Grams said. "But yes, part of the reason she had Emmett was so you would have a sibling."

"Why does it have to be so complicated?" I asked.

My grandmother smiled. "As I told you, Eloise, there's rarely black and white. Everything is complicated." I put my head down on the table and Grams rubbed my back. "Things tend to happen for a reason, Eloise. Maybe it's time. Have you told Emmett that you're thinking of looking for your father?"

"No," I said. "And I think he's going to flip."

chapter 10

I was right.

When I was sure that I was going to do it, that I was going to find my father, I called Emmett and told him there was something important I wanted to talk to him about.

"I don't need lectures from my big sister," he said. "If this is about Charla and the pregnancy, forget it. It's my business."

"It's not about Charla."

"Then what?"

"I don't want to get into it on the phone," I told him. "It's the kind of thing you talk about in person."

"What?" he said. "Just tell me."

"I'm going to find our father."

Silence.

"Emmett?"

"You're going to find that asshole?" he shouted. "Why? What the hell for?"

"Emmett, I don't want to talk about this on the phone," I said again. "Can you meet me for coffee? I'll come downtown."

"Fine," he muttered. "On the way down, think about what a bad idea it is to go find that loser, and by the time you show up, I'll be able to convince you not to do it."

When I arrived at a diner a few blocks away from Charla's apartment, Emmett was using his fork to poke at the ice cubes in his water glass.

"I ordered steak fries with gravy," he said.

I nodded.

"So, did the subway ride give you time to think?" he asked.

"Yes, it did. And now I'm a hundred and ten percent sure I should go find him."

That wasn't really true. I was really only forty percent sure I should try to find Theo Manfred.

"I can't believe you're going to find that asshole!" he shouted.

The elderly women in the booth in front of ours turned around and scowled.

Sorry, I mouthed to the one facing me.

"Emmett, could you not yell, please?"

"No, I can't not yell," he muttered. "What the hell are you doing? Why are you wasting your time going to look for someone who left you? Who didn't pay a dime in child support."

"Emmett, I told you why. It's something I need to do."

The waitress delivered his fries, and I ordered a cheese omelet.

His hazel eyes flashed with anger. "Why? Why do you *need* to do it?"

"Because it's unfinished business. I need to deal with it once and for all."

Emmett stabbed at a French fry and pointed it at me. "You don't *need* to, Eloise. The last thing you need is to find him. He doesn't deserve to be found."

"This isn't about him, Emmett. It's about me. I need some kind of closure. And maybe you do, too."

"Don't tell me what I need, okay?" he snapped.

"Okay. *I* need closure."

He raised an eyebrow. "From something that happened twenty-seven years ago?"

"Yes," I said. "Because it's still happening."

"What kind of psychobabble mumbo jumbo is that? It's still happening? Bullshit. If you have issues or whatever, it's not because of Theo Manfred."

"I'm going to find him, Emmett. I'm starting with Theodore L. Manfred in Pennsylvania, since that's where Grams says he's from. I know it's hard for you to deal with, but I need to do it for me. Just like you needed to do it when you were sixteen."

"I was a stupid teenager then," he said. "It's totally different. We're adults now."

Oh, really?

"Mom's probably turning over right now," Emmett muttered.

I glared at him. "I don't think so. Were she sitting right here, I think she'd support me."

"Well *I* don't support you," he said. He threw a ten-dollar bill on the table, grabbed his jacket and stomped out.

Yeah, Emmett. What else is new?

I was now the not-so-proud owner of a pair of yellow leather platform wedding shoes with a tiny tuft of yellow feathers on the ankle strap. After laughing at them for a full minute in Foot Couture on West Broadway (when the *Wow*ers were too busy kissing up to Astrid's awful taste), Jane oohed and aahed with the appropriate reverence for every click of Devlin's camera. My diary entry had to focus on how shopping for my wedding shoes differed from shopping for regular shoes. *Ooh, pick me—I know! It differs because I normally don't buy yellow shoes!*

Jane had hoped that a store that sold yellow platform shoes with feathers might also sell flag-inspired shoes, but no dice. When Astrid dismissed us, we hit a few likely stores, then gave up and decided to head uptown for our monthly candle-lighting ritual at St. Monica's.

We each lit a candle for our mothers. Jane picked up another candle to light for her father. "Why don't you light one for your father too?" she suggested.

"He's not dead," I reminded her.

"But he's gone," she said.

"But he's not dead."

"But he's gone," she repeated.

"He doesn't deserve a candle," I muttered, and walked over to the row of pews we always sat in, the very last.

Emmett was right about him not deserving.

"Eloise, the candle can be for the loss too," Jane whispered.

"Why does he deserve a candle?" I whispered back. "That would mean I care. That I think about him. That I give a flying shit."

"Sweetie, you're going to look for him tomorrow. I think you care."

I shook my head. "I'm going to look for him for *answers.* To put my past to rest. Not because I care about him."

"Okay, that's fair," she said. "But you're allowed to light the candle for *you*. For five-year-old Eloise whose fifth birthday really sucked. For six-year-old Eloise, seven-year-old Eloise, eight, nine, ten, eleven, twelve, thirteen—"

"Are you going to count all the way to thirty-two?" I asked her.

She nodded, and I smiled.

She squeezed my hand, then hung her head and stared at her feet, which meant she was thinking of her own father, of the last time she saw him. One day he'd been ball-room-dance-twirling her up Fifth Avenue to the Central Park Zoo, and the next day he was gone, senselessly, suddenly, suckily gone. She pulled a picture of her parents out of her purse and held it against her heart without looking at it.

I couldn't remember my father without pictures. I couldn't just conjure him up in my mind. When I did think of him, he would appear in my mind as he did in the few photos I had of him. A new wave haircut, a white button-down shirt. Jeans. Big black boots. That was him. He rarely smiled in the pictures.

There were some memories. Of candy stores. Of playgrounds. Of throwing me up in the air and catching me.

If he lived with us, I didn't remember anything, really.

"That's called repression," a shrink had once told me in college. I'd sought out a counselor in the crisis center when my breakup with my then-boyfriend, Michael, started affecting my ability to go to classes (I stopped for two weeks), or to eat or to come out from under the covers.

"It's not about the guy," the counselor had said. "I mean, it is, outwardly. But what it's triggering is your abandonment issue. Your father left you."

"I'm upset because the love of my life just dumped me," I yelled back.

"Wasn't your father once the love of your life?" the counselor countered.

Oh, please. Gut-boiling angry, I called him a quack and stormed out of his office.

I don't know if my father was the love of my life when I was five. I don't remember.

Apparently, that was called repression.

At the crack of dawn on Saturday morning, the phone rang.

Hi, Eloise, it's me, Noah. I've decided to stop being a traveling man. I'm staying home for good. You'll never have to see another at-the-ready bag again.

But it was Emmett. "Don't leave without me," he said. "I'll be there in a half hour." *Click.*

Well, well.

I sat up in bed and grabbed Noah's pillow and held it to my chest and breathed in the soapy scent of him. This weekend he was *Hot News*ing in Colorado with Call Me Ash. A UFO had been spotted by several residents of a small town—the mayor included.

I didn't know how to pack, how long we'd be away, what to put in my purse. I only knew I was going to Pennsylvania, to the address I'd found on the Internet.

I decided to bring nothing but the directions. That way, I wouldn't have expectations of staying overnight—or not.

What did you wear to meet your father for the first time in twenty-seven years? Should I flatten my hair as befitted the Modern Bride or poof it up as befitted my usual self?

I settled on a black turtleneck, a denim knee-length skirt, my most comfortable low-heeled black knee-high boots and a little makeup. I let my hair do whatever it did when I stepped out of the shower. I looked like me.

A half hour later, Emmett and Charla were at my front door, carrying overnight bags. Clearly they had expectations. Or were just prepared for anything.

Emmett looked tired; Charla looked excited.

For someone who wasn't committed, Emmett sure brought Charla everywhere—and everywhere important.

Emmett dropped his bag and ran a hand through his hair. "I want to come with you so that when we find him, I can punch him out and go back home and get on with my fucking life."

Charla patted his shoulder. "I convinced Emmett that he has some residual anger where his father is concerned," she whispered, as though Emmett couldn't hear her.

"I'm not angry," he said.

"But you want to beat up our father?" I said.

He picked up his bag and slung it over his shoulder. "Would you stop calling him 'our father'? He's not 'our father.' He's our *biological* father."

No, Emmett, you're not angry.

chapter 11

Emmett was staring out the back-seat window of our rented beige Chevy, grim-faced as usual. Charla was singing "This Land Is Your Land." And I was biting the inside of my lip and counting trees. I'd gotten up to five hundred million. Having been a city kid all my life, I'd never seen so many trees in a row. For the past twenty minutes, there had been nothing but trees. Highway and trees and the occasional green sign indicating where the heck we were. Weigh Station. Next exit 14 miles. Speed Limit: 55 (and sometimes 65).

We'd been driving for an hour and a half and were still in New Jersey. I had no idea New Jersey was so pretty. Given all the jokes about "which exit" and smokestacks and Jersey Girls, whodathunk there were acres and acres of untouched land, snowy white and unpolluted by eight million people and eight million taxi cabs. I saw more cows and horses in the half hour than I'd seen in my entire life.

We were on our way to Boonsonville, Pennsylvania, population 4,600, which, according to Yahoo Maps, was in Bucks County. My grandmother thought Bucks County, with its historic towns and artsy, charming, woodsy atmosphere, fit with what she remembered of Theodore Leo Manfred, Writer. According to Facts About Boonsonville, if you lived in town, either the historical district or downtown, you could get along without a car if you were the type who could. From what my grandmother told me and the little my mother mentioned over the years, Theo Manfred was the type who would get along without a car.

We didn't exactly have a plan about what we were going to do when we got there. We had a name that matched, a state that matched and an address. That was where we were headed.

"Are we just gonna knock on the door and see if a man resembling us opens it?" Emmett asked.

"I guess," I said.

"You've really planned this out," he said.

I ignored him.

"I've been to Pennsylvania before," Charla chirped. "When I was a kid, we went on a school field trip to see the Liberty Bell. And I've also been to Hershey Park. It's like a chocolate wonderland. God, I miss chocolate!"

Emmett reached into his pocket and handed her a Snickers bar.

She beamed but wagged her finger at it. "Chocolate contains caffeine. The baby can't have any."

Emmett paled and took back the candy bar.

I tried to imagine how Emmett felt about the baby, but I couldn't. I had no idea how he felt about *Charla*. Four years? And he'd never even mentioned her? How was that possible? If I hadn't gotten a glimpse of her myself last year in my doorway, I wouldn't have known she even existed.

"I have no idea how I'm going to get along without coffee," Charla said. "I can't have coffee, chocolate, farmed salmon, tuna, swordfish—"

Emmett looked at her quizzically. "Fish has caffeine?" he asked.

"Mercury," she said.

"Oh," he said.

"I can't have soft cheese or bacon either," she added.

Emmett nodded again, and that was the extent of his contribution to the conversation.

I peered at Charla in the rearview mirror. She was trying very hard. For the first hour, she'd steered clear of pregnancy talk, but Emmett hadn't responded any better. From the moment we put on our seat belts and pulled out of the garage, Charla had tried her best to lighten up the tension. She'd tried chatting ("So, were you two close as kids?") and games ("How many girls' first names can you come up with that start with the letter V?") and then a running monologue about how many deer are hit on rural highways.

Finally, Emmett handed me a CD. Charla announced that it was her favorite, which got her smiling and Emmett what he wanted, which was her silence.

I popped it into the player. I could take the noise for about a minute, then turned on the radio instead.

"You always had bad taste in music," Emmett said. "Totally commercial stuff."

"I could sing," Charla suggested, and before we could say, *No, that's really okay,* she launched into folk favorites. She'd finished "This Land Is Your Land" and was now on "Blowin' In the Wind."

She stopped singing. "I really have to pee," she said.

She really had to pee a lot. Apparently, pregnant women went to the bathroom every twenty minutes. Between the last two rest stops, she'd explained exactly what pressed on the bladder.

"I think it's the baby's tush," she said.

"Victor," Emmett said fast before she could elaborate.

"What, honey?" Charla asked.

"Names that start with V."

She laughed. "Okay, I'll change the subject. But Victor isn't a girl's name."

"Victoria," he said.

I laughed spontaneously, and we caught eyes in the rearview mirror. He looked away.

Our mother used to play the name game with Emmett and me. Emmett and I would come up with names she'd never heard of, like Danae (there were two in my sixth-grade class), and our mother would challenge us with names we'd never heard of, like Gertrude and Milt.

"I can barely hold it in," Charla managed to say as I pulled onto the service road leading to a McDonald's. "Maybe it's the baby's head pressing against my bladder—"

"Vera," Emmett said. "Vanessa. Valerie. Vania."

I laughed, but if you thought about it, it really wasn't funny at all.

Twenty-five minutes later, Charla needed to stop again.

"How do you feel about the pregnancy?" I asked Emmett as she disappeared inside another McDonald's.

"I don't want to talk about it," he said.

Hey, that was my line.

Forty minutes later, we were lost and Charla needed to stop again.

She held the map up to her face. "I can't even concentrate on this tiny type. I have to go sooooo bad!"

"Emmett, can you figure out where we are and how to get back on the highway?" I asked him.

He had his headphones on. Charla nudged him. He took them off and grudgingly took the map. He peered out the window for a street sign.

"Make a left," he said. "And just keep going."

I did, and signs for the highway appeared.

So that was what constant travel was good for.

According to Emmett, we were now in the same Mc-Donald's we were in a half hour ago.

When you were born, raised and lived in New York City and didn't have a car (7.5 million of the population?), you had to rent one when you needed to go anywhere. Highways, maps, rest stops were all new to me.

Charla came back to the car eating a McVeggie burger and slurping a vanilla shake.

"Ready?" I asked the two of them.

Emmett put on his headphones and closed his eyes. No one could ever accuse him of being a side-seat driver.

"Want some company?" Charla asked, nodding at the passenger seat. "Chatty here is giving me an earache."

I laughed. "Sure."

A moment later we were back on the highway, this time headed in the right direction.

Exit: Boonsonville. One and a half miles.

I now knew what a rush of blood to the head felt like. My heart started pounding. *Boom. Boom. Boom.* How could Charla not hear it? *Boom. Boom. Boom.*

But she was talking about baby names she liked. Thelonious for a boy.

Thelonious? Was that a name?

"I wouldn't use a name that started with 'The,'" I said. "Bad luck."

"Huh?"

"Our father's name is Theodore," I pointed out.

"Ah. But do you like the name Thelonious?" she asked. "I think it's really musical and meaningful."

I glanced at her to see if she was kidding, but she wasn't. Charla's expression was perpetually hopeful, almost too sincere.

"Honestly?" I asked.

She nodded. "It's a mouthful. Maybe a better name for a musician than a baby."

"I also like Mike," she said.

I laughed. "From Thelonious to Mike, huh?"

"Emmett likes the name Finn."

That surprised me. "You and Emmett have discussed baby names?"

"Not really," she said. "I mean, I have, and he usually says, 'Charl, you're only *ten* weeks pregnant.' But a few days ago, I asked him how he felt about the name Lorenzo and he said—"

She burst into tears.

I pulled over. We both glanced back at Emmett; he was lightly snoring.

I handed her a tissue.

She blew her nose and sniffled. "He said Lorenzo Gould sounded really dumb."

Oh. Meaning Emmett was so mentally out of the picture as the baby's father that he didn't even *assume* Charla would give the child his name.

"Give him a little time," I told her. "He's only known for what, a couple of weeks? Maybe when he gets used to the idea he'll start saying Lorenzo *Manfred* sounds dumb."

"He'll be hitchhiking his way to Texas by then," she said. "He likes the idea of trying out Austin. He says there's a great music scene there."

"I wouldn't worry about that," I assured her. "Vegetarians don't move to cattle country."

She brightened for a split second. "That's true! El, I'm really sorry, but I really have to pee again."

"There's an exit coming up any minute. I'm sure there will be a rest stop."

"We passed the last exit ten minutes ago," she said. "Didn't you see the sign that said Next Exit, 14 miles?"

Nope, I hadn't.

"And that was the exit we needed," I said. "Boonsonville."

"Some say there are no accidents," she pointed out.

"I don't think there are," I told her.

"I could go for a burger," Emmett said at the next rest stop. "Anyone want anything?"

Charla burst into tears.

So much for being a vegetarian.

"Hormones," I told him. "She'll be okay. Go ahead. We're fine."

He looked at Charla, chewed his lip for a second, then ambled off toward the rest stop.

Two women in a little blue car smiled after him; one of them wolf-whistled. He didn't even turn around.

I took off my seat belt. "Come on, Charla. Let's hit the bathrooms just in case you need to go. I can ask for directions back to the exit."

"'Kay," she said, wiping her eyes.

Five minutes later, bathroomed, face-splashed and ginger-aled, we sat at a picnic bench, rubbing our hands together. It was cold. Thirty-seven degrees and overcast.

"I'm freezing," I said. "Want to head back to the car?"

"My father bailed on me too," Charla said suddenly.

I glanced at her. "Really?"

She nodded and took a sip of her soda. "He fell in love with someone else and that was that. He left when I was seven, moved to Oregon and I never saw him again until I went looking for him when I was twenty."

"You found him?"

She nodded.

"I have a half brother and a half sister."

I hadn't thought of that. Did Emmett and I have half brothers and half sisters?

"What happened when you found him?" I asked.

"He acted all happy to see me, but it was more like I was a distant relative he'd met a few times and liked—and one he expected to go home and call in a few months or something. The whole thing was really disappointing. I guess I'm glad I found him, but it didn't make me feel better."

I looked at her. Her nose was red from crying, from the cold. "So why did you push Emmett to come with me?"

"Because it's something you both need to do to move past a hump."

She shook her head. "I feel like, if he'll just confront this—" She started to cry.

I didn't know what to say. She'd already been through the hardest part of what I was just beginning to do. I covered her hand with mine.

"It's not that I think he'll find his dad and suddenly have closure and be able to move on and settle down and marry me and be father of the year," she said. "But a girl can dream, right?" She let out a deep breath. "I love him so much."

I suddenly realized how misguided it was to judge other people's relationships. If I weren't Emmett's sister but just a friend of Charla's, I might have said, *Why? Or… How could you love someone so immature? Someone who's not even all that nice to you?*

But I knew how. I loved Emmett, too. Only because he was my brother? I didn't think so. I loved him because I *knew* him. Yes, we were family. But blood and love could be mutually exclusive. My father had taught me that.

"It's good that he's here," she said. "That you're both here. Yeah, I think he's going to be a huge mess that I'm going to have to deal with while I'm pregnant. I think it's going to be very raw and very ugly for him. But do you just repress this kind of loss and pain and live like Emmett, or do you face it head-on like *you're* willing to do? Like you're *doing.*"

Suddenly I wasn't sure whether it was worth it or not. Was it so terrible to repress pain and loss that you couldn't do anything about? Was it so terrible to accept the shitty, gritty reality that our father had left us and go about our lives as best we could? What were we supposed to do? Spend tens of thousands of dollars on therapists? Just accept and forget it? Go find him and demand answers?

How did you know?

I was here and I still didn't know.

"I've been thinking about the job your boss offered me" came Emmett's voice.

Startled, Charla and I whirled around. I had no idea how long Emmett had been standing there. He was holding a McDonald's bag in one hand and a shake in the other. He'd left his jacket in the car, and his cheeks were red from the cold.

"Oh?" I said.

"Five hundred bucks is five hundred bucks, right?" he said. "Charla will need it to buy some stuff for the baby."

Charla pressed a hand to her mouth. She flew up to hug him, and he awkwardly embraced her.

"I want to go home," Emmett said to me. "Maybe next weekend we'll try again, but I want to get out of here."

I looked at him and nodded.

I wanted to go home too. We'd been gone four hours, and I'd never been so homesick in my life.

Noah was home. When I opened the door to our apartment, there he was, sprawled on the couch, watching a hockey game and reading *Newsweek,* a giant-size red-foil-wrapped pair of chocolate lips on the coffee table.

I ran into his arms. "But you're in Colorado!"

"Actually, I'm right here," he said as he took off my coat, trailing kisses down my neck and arms.

"But you're on staking out aliens in the mayor's backyard!"

"Ashley's in the mayor's backyard," he corrected. "*I'm* in my yard."

Mayor, my name's Ashley, but you can call me Ash, because you're the mayor and because I smolder…

I could see the headlines now: *Hot News Reporter Noah Benjamin investigating the scandalous love affair between his former colleague, known only as Call Me Ash, and the mayor. Call Me Ash torn between hot Hot News colleague and UFO-spotting local politician.*

"But I thought you weren't coming home till Sunday night or even Monday night," I said.

He pulled me next to him on the couch. "I wanted to be here when you got home. What you're doing is tough stuff, and a phone call between us long-distance wasn't going to cut it."

"You came home just so you'd be here when I got home?"

He nodded. "And I got you this. Valentine's Day goodies hit the stores early in the Midwest."

He picked up the giant chocolate lips and pressed them to mine.

I laughed. "I don't even know how to say thanks. Thanks isn't enough."

"It's always enough," he said. "Anyway, I'm not that selfless. I also came back because I missed you."

Top Ten List for World's Best Boyfriend and Fiancé and Husband-To-Be: #1: Noah Benjamin.

I kissed him. "I missed you, too."

"How'd the trip go?" he asked.

"It didn't. I mean, we didn't even find the town he lives in. We never even left the highway, well, except for making wrong turns out of rest stops. We did get to experience many different McDonald's, though."

"How'd you and Emmett get along?"

"Like siblings," I said.

He smiled. "I've never spent five agreeable minutes with Beth in a car. Not when we were kids and not now."

I couldn't imagine spending five agreeable minutes with Beth anywhere, and I wasn't her sibling. Though I suppose soon enough, I sort of would be.

"Charla was a surprise, though," I said. "I like her."

"C'mere," he said, massaging my shoulders. "Sit back and tell me all about it from start to finish."

"You know what I would rather do?"

"What?"

I took off his T-shirt.

"And miss the hockey game?" he teased, grabbing the remote control and clicking off the TV.

"I love you, Noah," I said. "I really, really love you."

"Me, too," he said, trailing kisses across my belly button.

I will stop twisting my ring on my finger. Noah is the man for me. Noah is the greatest boyfriend and fiancé in the world. It's nice to come home to someone you love when you've spent the day with your stomach muscles clenched and your heart in your throat. It's nice to come home to Valentine's Day chocolate in January.

The good news for me was that for the first time in a long time, I was scared of something else.

chapter 12

"Fine. Whatever!" Philippa was muttering into her phone when I arrived at work on Monday morning. "Fine!" she yelled again. "Well then, I don't care either!" She slammed down the phone, then picked it up and slammed it down three more times.

I poked my head over the rim of her cubicle. "Are you okay?"

She nodded, but her eyes filled with tears and her lips trembled.

I came around and sat down in her guest chair. "Did you and Parker just get into a fight?"

She shook her head.

I couldn't imagine what else could have gone wrong in Philippa Wills's charmed life. Barneys wasn't having its semiannual sale? Her hairstylist was going on vacation and she needed a trim?

Devlin's assistant poked her head in, said, "Hot off the

press!" and handed Philippa a manila folder. "Your father-daughter shots. They're terrific. Devlin is showing them to Astrid right now."

I expected Philippa to lunge for the folder and rip it open, but she didn't budge. Neither did her expression. She was on the verge of tears again.

"Philippa, what's wrong?" I asked.

She sniffled.

"Philippa, if you—"

Devlin's assistant coughed. "Uh, Eloise, you're needed in the conference room for a layout meeting."

"Will you be all right till I come back?" I asked Philippa.

She managed a shaky nod, then stared down at her desk.

"You sure?"

She nodded. "I'm okay. Go ahead. Really."

But the second I left her cubicle, I heard her try to stifle a squeaky sob.

Unless someone else on the *Wow Weddings* staff wore pink wingtip oxfords, Philippa Wills was in the middle stall of the women's rest room, crying.

Whatever was bothering her was *really* bothering her. I'd been trapped in a design meeting on the Grooms-and-Fathers-To-Be feature for an hour and a half.

"Philippa, it's me, Eloise."

Silence. Rustle of toilet paper.

"Philippa? Are you okay?"

Sniffle. Nose blow. "Just allergies," she finally said.

And then she burst into tears.

"Philippa, open up. Let me in."

Silence.

A moment later, she unlatched the stall door, and I squeezed in. Her beautiful peaches-and-cream skin was ruddy, and her eyes were red-rimmed from crying. She was sitting on the lid of the toilet, a wad of pink tissues in her lap.

"Philippa, maybe I can help. Did you get into a fight with Parker? It's all right if you did. All couples fight and—"

She shook her head. "We didn't get into a fight."

"Astrid say something evil?"

Again, a head shake. "Astrid's been really nice to me lately. She even stopped by my cubicle a little while ago to tell me that my family is the ultimate in Classic and that my father-daughter shots were spectacular. She said if she were giving grades for family, I'd get an A plus."

Once again, *I* wouldn't get a grade.

She burst into sobs again, burying her face in the tissues.

And you're in here crying because…

"Then what's wrong, Philippa?"

"Nothing. Forget it." She stood up and blew her nose again, then burst into tears and sank back down.

Perhaps she wanted privacy. "Do you want me to leave you alone?"

She grabbed my hand. "Will you sneak out with me for coffee? I don't want to talk about it here."

Five minutes later, we were in Starbucks with peppermint mochas and a cinnamon-chip scone to split. We sat in upholstered chairs at a little round table, letting the warmth and sweetness of our coffee relax us for a moment. The attractive man at the next table was sneaking appreciative peeks at Philippa, but she didn't notice.

Even with red-rimmed eyes, Philippa elicited stares.

Because I saw her every day, I stopped noticing how striking she was. When I interviewed at *Wow Weddings* and Philippa stepped into the reception area to fetch me to Astrid's office because Astrid's assistant was out that day, I'd been momentarily dumbstruck. And intimidated. Not by her, personally, but by the way she looked and dressed. I didn't look or dress anything like the Gwyneth Paltrow perfection that was Philippa Wills.

Five foot ten, thin as a rail, with poker-straight white-blond hair, the headband, the shirtwaist dress and penny loafers, maybe a dusting of blush and a little lip gloss, Philippa Wills, editorial assistant, was bursting with enthusiasm (she'd bubbled nonstop from the moment she collected me until she deposited me in Astrid's toile-covered guest chair about what a wonderful working environment *Wow Weddings* was, even if you weren't engaged, which she wasn't, by the way, and etcetera, etcetera).

At Posh Publishing, where I'd worked for eight years, bubbling with enthusiasm was about as welcome as a buzzing fly.

Philippa hadn't lost that bubble in the little over two years she'd been working at *Wow.* And if Acid hadn't popped it out of her yet...

Which made a sad, crying Philippa very difficult to bear.

"Philippa, you can trust me, okay?" I assured her. "Whatever it is."

She sniffled into her tissue. "I trust you. But I can't tell you."

"Well, how about if we just sit here and enjoy our coffee, then," I said. "Maybe this scone will make you feel better."

She broke off a piece but didn't eat it. "I want to tell you. I really do. But I'm so embarrassed."

"Hey, who's the queen of embarrassing herself at *Wow?*"

"You are," she said earnestly.

"So therefore," I reasoned at my own expense, "you can tell me. No matter what it is, I'm sure I've topped it."

"You won't tell a soul?" she asked. "Not a soul?"

"Cross my heart," I assured her.

"Not even Noah?"

"Not even Noah," I promised.

She let out a deep breath and gnawed her lower lip. "My family hates me."

"Your family hates you?" I repeated. "Philippa, your father thinks you're the greatest thing that ever walked the earth. Your mother adores you, and your brother is your best friend."

"Not really," she whispered.

"Philippa, I was at your photo shoot," I reminded her. "Your father couldn't stop talking about how great you are. You and your brother couldn't decide which one of you was the 'best.' And your mother—"

"They were paid to do all that," she finally said.

Huh? "You paid your family to say nice—"

Oh.

She stared down at her feet. "They're not my family. They're stand-ins. Fakes. Models I hired from Perfect People."

No wonder the fake Weston Wills looked familiar! I'd probably seen his head shot when I was looking for my own fake brother.

"They're costing me two hundred fifty an hour," she said between sniffles. "My stand-in brother goes for three hundred, because he's particularly hot right now."

My fake brother would have cost only one hundred and seventy-five.

"You hired models because you're not getting along with your family?" I asked.

Silence.

"Philippa, trust me—I'm the last person who'll judge you about family."

She glanced up at me and gnawed her lip, then took a sip of her coffee. "Not getting along is an understatement. They totally hate me."

Philippa was a lot of things, but hateable wasn't among them. "Why do you think they hate you?"

"My parents and brother are boycotting my wedding," she said in such a low voice I had to lean forward, which meant I was almost in her lap. "And anything to do with the magazine feature."

I waited for her to continue.

Because...

"They totally hate me," she said on a sob.

Because...

"Because I...sort of shortened my last name when I graduated from college."

From...what? Willspimple? Willsfart? Willssnot?

"Wilschitz," she said.

Ah. Wilschitz. I would have gotten there eventually.

"A lot of people shorten their names," I told her. "Have you tried ex—"

"I changed my first name too," she added.

I waited.

"It used to be—"

I was on the edge of my seat.

"Phyllis," she finally said.

Phyllis Wilschitz.

Philippa Wills's real name was Phyllis Wilschitz.

"My family says I'm pretending to be something I'm

not, but that's not true!" she said. "I am Philippa Wills! Philippa Wills is who I was meant to be."

"Who was Phyllis Wilschitz?" I asked.

She let out a deep breath. "When I walked down the hall in middle school, boys would shout out, 'Run, everybody—Phyllis Will Shit!' And girls would add, 'Phyllis *Is* Shit!'"

"Oh, God, Philippa. How awful."

I was surprised though. Usually girls who looked like Philippa were immune to middle-school torture. Philippa Wills (or Phyllis Wilschitz) had never had a pimple, let alone a bad hair day. It just wasn't possible.

"I wasn't exactly as pulled together then as I am now. I was a walking stereotype—the Coke-bottle glasses, bad posture from hunching over because I towered over all the boys, bad hair, the works."

Ah. I peered at her. It was impossible even to imagine.

She took a sip of her coffee. "But my parents were sticking me in a private school for high school and I realized I had a shot at changing my image."

"By changing your name to something glamorous?" I asked. "Glam by association?"

"Actually, back then I didn't realize I could change my name," she said. "I changed how I *looked*. I turned Phyllis Wilschitz into a hot babe."

"How?"

"I read through every back issue of *Teen* and *Seventeen,* then bought Miss Clairol Light Blond, a pair of contact lenses and inexpensive versions of stylish clothing that I saw in *Seventeen* and on the popular girls at school. I practiced applying my new stockpile of cosmetics, stood up straight like my then idol Cindy Crawford and *voilà*."

"Your parents helped you do all this?" I asked. "They

let you change your whole look in high school but have problems with your name?"

"Oh, they didn't help me," she said. "I had some money saved from birthdays and holidays and every baby-sitting job I ever had. My mother was furious when she saw my dyed hair. She insisted I change it back. I begged her to understand."

"Did she?" I asked.

"She took a pair of scissors and cut off my hair."

I literally gasped. "She did not!"

"Yup, she did. She said that no daughter of hers was going to walk around like a harlot with bleached-blond hair when she and my father scrimped and saved to get me into private school."

Scrimped and saved? I thought her parents were wealthy.

"So she cut off my long hair to my chin and told me it would grow out faster if it was short," Philippa continued, "but then she didn't want people to think I'd colored my hair, so she kept dyeing it for me. I got to be blond with a chic bob all through high school."

"Wow," I said.

"I was still Phyllis Wilschitz, but I looked like a Philippa Wills. And I was treated accordingly. I was never made fun of again, but I hated the name. *Hated* it. I tried to explain that to my parents when I changed my name after college, that the name Phyllis Wilschitz didn't match the new me. That I needed a name that conjured up an image of money, class, beauty, elegance."

"Let me guess," I said. "They were more than a little insulted."

She nodded.

"Even so, I'm sure they don't *hate* you. And there's no

way they'd miss their girl getting married. I'm sure they won't boycott the wedding."

Philippa started to cry again. "I don't know. They're *really* mad at me. They say that Wills is a slap in the face to them. That my father's name, my grandfather's name, my great-grandfather's name, my great-great-grandfather's name ain't Wills. It's Wilschitz. Every time I get the lecture, they really emphasize the *schitz*. Wil-*schitz!* Wil-*schitz!* Don't they know that only strengthens my resolve to be Wills?"

"Did your brother get teased?" I asked.

If you even have a brother.

She nodded. "He was tortured. Mercilessly. And it affected him his entire life. When you're teased that way, picked on, made fun of every single day so carelessly, you either turn into a raging lunatic or you retreat. My brother retreated."

"So he's not Mr. Wall Street?"

She smiled. "He's a librarian."

"Does he understand about your changing your name?"

She shook her head. "He didn't change his. But then again, his first name is Mike. That's livable."

"You really think they'll boycott the wedding?" I asked.

"They figured I'd stop 'this name nonsense,' my last name, anyway, when I married Parker. They assumed I'd become Philippa Gersh and they'd never have to see or hear the Wills again. But I'm not taking Parker's name and—"

I was surprised. Very. "You're not taking Parker's name?"

"Why should I?" she asked.

"No reason. I guess I just assumed."

"I worked really hard to become Philippa Wills. I'm not going to give up who I am just because I'm getting married. And who I am is Philippa Wills. I'm not Phyllis Wilschitz or Philippa Gersh. I'm Philippa Wills."

I was impressed. Very. "Good for you, Philippa," I said. "So what does Parker think of all this?"

She gnawed her lower lip.

"Philippa, Parker does know your real name, doesn't he?"

She didn't answer.

Whoo-boy.

She sipped her coffee. "What was the point of telling him? We'd been dating only four months when Parker proposed, so it was too early for a 'meet the folks,' and since he proposed there hasn't been an opportunity to get all of us together. I haven't *had* to tell him. I'll tell him before I introduce him to the Wilschitzes. Whenever that will be…"

"But you *will* have to eventually because—" *Your name is really Phyllis Wilschitz.*

"Because why? Because Philippa Wills isn't really my name?" she asked. "It is. It's as much my name as if my parents had named me that twenty-five years ago. I'm Philippa Wills."

But—

But what? Was she wrong?

I tried to imagine telling Noah that my name wasn't really Eloise Manfred.

Me: "Noah, before we get married, there's something I have to tell you. My name isn't really Eloise Manfred. It's Elowishious Manfrednoodle."

Noah: "What? You lying liar! You're not who said you were. It's over. We're breaking up. The wedding is off!" Yanks ring off finger and stomps away.

If I told Noah that my real name were Elowishious

Manfrednoodle, I had no doubt he'd really say, "Thank God you changed it. I wouldn't have gone on a first date with you if your name were Elowishious Manfrednoodle."

Then again, Elowishious Manfrednoodle wasn't a name anyone would have.

I tried to imagine Philippa telling Parker Gersh that her real name was Phyllis Wilschitz.

Parker: "Phyllis Wilschitz? How are we supposed to get our wedding announcement in the *New York Times* with a name like Phyllis Wilschitz? I can see the headline now: Instead of Philippa Will Marry, it'll say Phyllis Will Shit."

Or: "Phyllis Wilschitz? We *are* a match made in heaven! My real name is Phallus Gershhead."

I didn't know Parker Gersh well; I didn't know him at all, actually. I'd met him only once, on his and Philippa's first date. Noah and I had arranged it as a double date after work. Philippa had rushed into the *Wow* rest room at exactly 5:00 p.m. with her cosmetics kit, curling iron, straightening iron, hair spray, perfume and three different outfits, including the one she was wearing.

Two seconds after we arrived at the restaurant, a busboy spilled my glass of red wine all over Philippa's dress. Parker snapped unnecessarily at the busboy, but he was beyond gracious to Philippa, running to the bar to ask for a little seltzer and napkins, assuring her she still looked remarkably beautiful and would were she wearing a burlap sack. Philippa had beamed and let down her guard and that, as they say, was that.

He'd adored her from minute one and had treated her like a princess since. Philippa was right. Why would he care that her last name didn't match his? What did it matter what your name was? Didn't we all learn in eleventh-grade English class that a rose by any other name would still smell as sweet?

Then again, Emmett had learned the opposite. He'd changed his name for two weeks when he was in high school.

"Why should I have the last name of someone I haven't seen since I was two?" he'd said in angry defense of his newly chosen last name, Smith, after his then hero, Robert Smith of the alternative-rock band The Cure. Unfortunately, *Emmett* wasn't an uncommon name in New York City; there were four Emmetts in his English class alone and two in his history class, and he didn't get credit for homework he'd turned in or reports or tests, and my grandmother had to come in for a meeting with his guidance counselor and the principal. Emmett had to make up the homework and reports and tests he'd turned in as Emmett Smith, despite the fact that his teachers still had the original work. Apparently, if the work didn't have Emmett's real name on it, he couldn't get credit.

It seemed so silly then, and even sillier now. Emmett Smith's book report wasn't (according to the school), *really* written by Emmett Manfred because it had another student's name on it (despite the fact that there was no Emmett Smith enrolled), even if it really was. So if Phyllis Wilschitz's name was on the marriage license, would Philippa Wills really be married?

What *did* it matter what your name was? My mother's last name had never been Manfred—she and my father had never married. Did the fact that she had a different last name than me and Emmett make her any less my mother? Did the fact that I had the same name as a man I hadn't seen since I was five make him any more my father?

I'd always planned on taking my husband's name—the

perfect opportunity to ditch the Manfred that I never felt connected to in the first place. But Emmett was a Manfred. His child would be a Manfred, even if he or she were named Gould. Unless, of course, he or she changed it to something else in eleventh grade.

Eloise Benjamin.

That was the first time I put the two names together. Who the hell was Eloise Benjamin?

chapter 13

After she'd assured me she was all right, that she just needed to think and sip her peppermint mocha, I finally left Philippa at Starbucks and headed for the subway. I was meeting Noah and the *Wow* staff at Round Rings for the wedding-rings "selection." As the train zoomed and shook and rumbled its way downtown, I took out the red leather journal book Jane had given me as a New Year's gift and wrote *Eloise Benjamin*.

Didn't feel right. No, that wasn't it. The name didn't feel *familiar*. Didn't look familiar.

I tried script. Print. Calligraphy. (I took a course two years ago during my hiatus from dating.)

Eloise Benjamin. Eloise Benjamin. Eloise Benjamin.

I rummaged through my bag for a Tums. I popped two in my mouth and wrote *Eloise Manfred*.

Yes, that was right.

Okay, fine, I was Eloise Manfred, but I was marrying

Noah Benjamin, so even, say, spiritually, when we became one, I would become Eloise Benjamin.

I wrote *Eloise Benjamin.* And needed another Tums.

I put away the journal book and stared up at the advertisements lining the top rim of the subway car.

"That means you don't want to get married."

I glanced up to find a middle-aged woman sitting next to me pointing at my ring. "When you tug at it like that," she added, "it's supposed to mean you don't want to get married."

Mind your own stupid business, I wanted to yell, but luckily, the doors opened and I fled onto the Spring Street platform.

Why, after last night, wonderful, delicious, orgasmic last night, was I back to twisting my ring? Just because I wasn't yet used to Eloise Benjamin?

Eloise Benjamin. Eloise Benjamin. Eloise Benjamin.

What was the big deal? It was my first name and my fiancé's last name. Put 'em together you got Eloise Benjamin.

I popped another Tums.

What was my problem? It couldn't be the name, since I didn't *have* to change my name—even though I wanted to. It couldn't be the guy, since I *wanted* to marry him— or I had until he proposed, anyway.

Unless it was the guy.

Was it Noah?

The man in question arrived at Round Rings at exactly the same time as I did. I, from the north, and he from the south.

"Jinx," he said, kissing me.

That had to mean something, arriving at the ring shop at exactly the same time from opposite directions. There had to be something yin and yang about that.

"Your lips are cold," I told him, closing my eyes as he hugged me.

I will not twist my ring anymore. I will not twist my ring anymore. I will not twist my ring anymore. It isn't Noah. It's not him, it's me.

Hey, wait a minute. *It's not you, it's me* meant it *was* him! The moment we entered the shop, everyone turned around to check out the Modern Bride's fiancé. "Um, everyone," I said. "This is my fiancé, Noah Benjamin."

Noah gave a little wave to the gaggle of *Wow*ers.

Devlin eyed him up and down. "We'll have to lose the Burberry. The Modern Bride's fiancé needs to be strictly metrosexual."

There were once-overs and nods, and in less than a minute, Noah's heavy tan trench coat was replaced by the proprietor's black suede jacket. Devlin offered Noah his ridiculous eyeglasses, which the King of Pretentious confessed were for show only when Noah pointed out that his vision was twenty-twenty.

Devlin wrinkled his nose at Noah's pants. "We'll shoot from the waist up. The black pants are okay, but they're a little too 'midtown.'"

Devlin was lucky that Noah wasn't the type to punch him out.

Astrid was picking over every inch of Noah. "All right, Groom of the Modern Bride. Let's have a look at you. Spin around twice, please."

Noah spun. As a guy who staked out UFOs in mayors' backyards, Noah couldn't possibly be surprised by anyone. Acid O'Connor, in her minuscule eyeglasses and orange cashmere wrap, barely fazed him.

She eyed him from head to toe, stopping midsection to peer at his tie—many tiny Morticia Addamses today.

"Yes, I would say you're now Modern Bride-worthy," Astrid affirmed.

Well, well. The tie got to stay. Score one for Morticia.

The proprietor was beaming. "It's my pleasure to welcome *Wow Weddings* to Round Rings Jewelry Emporium. We're delighted to be participating in the magazine's Today's Bride feature. And to that end, we've selected two display cases that feature rings we feel best reflect our ring salon and the clientele we'd like to cultivate."

He placed the cases onto the tiniest desk I'd ever seen. Noah and I and the *Wow* staff crowded around and peered at the rings.

"This case is hers and that case is his," the man said.

If he hadn't made that distinction, I wouldn't have known the difference.

Noah eyed the rings in the *his* case. "Is that rust?" he whispered to me.

"I don't think so," I said.

"It's a special finishing process," the proprietor said, pronouncing the "o" in *process* like *pro.* "It's one of our most popular bands."

Noah coughed. "I was thinking something simple. Gold or silver, simple band."

The proprietor looked at him quizzically. "We don't do *simple,* sir."

In Noah's display case were twelve rings, one more bizarre than the next. There was a rusted zigzag. A square with tiny diamonds that spelled out *peace.* A triangle whose point hit the knuckle.

No. No. And more no.

It was one thing to have the word Peace spelled out on a veil I'd wear for a few hours; it was another to have it on the wedding ring I'd wear for the rest of my life.

"Um, I can't see these going with my engagement ring," I said.

The proprietor didn't blink. "Don't you worry about that—you'll simply move your ring to your right hand. That's what brides do when they fall madly in love with a ring that doesn't blend with their diamond."

I had to restrain myself from laughing in his face.

Noah held up a thin square band with an inlet of bronze. "I guess this one is okay."

The proprietor looked disappointed. "It's our most traditional piece, but if it's what you like…"

"I'll take the bride's version," I said.

Astrid sighed. "Perhaps the Modern Bride and her groom can take another look at the displays."

The Modern Bride has seen enough.

I feigned a look at the rings and picked up the hers version of Noah's. "Yes indeedy, this is my choice. You, Noah?"

"I'm very happy with the one I picked," he said.

The proprietor nodded. "The selections are fine with me. The rings may be our least avant-garde, yet they're sure to lure modern brides to our Web site and to visit our shops nationwide."

Ha! Sure to lure modern brides anywhere but *Round Rings.*

"Um, what metal is this, anyway?" I asked.

The proprietor smiled. "It's a special blend of metals."

"Whoa," Noah said, peering at the tiny sticker inside the ring. "This ring is nine thousand dollars?"

"The bride's is twelve thousand, seven hundred," said the proprietor.

But I could have found this myself at the scrap yard.

"I've saved the best news for last," Astrid announced. "We've secured two celebrities to model a selection of Round Rings for the feature!"

"Fabulous," the proprietor exclaimed with a little clap of his hands, and off he and Astrid went to sign papers.

But we hate these rings, I wanted to yell at them. We have to wear these for the rest of our lives and we hate them!

Devlin and his assistant began setting up their equipment. "Okay, Modern Bride and Groom. Let's shoot a roll with you two entering the shop, expectant smiles on your faces. You'll beeline straight for the display case and both reach for Eloise's ring at the same time, making happy, surprised faces. You'll then ooh and aah at the ring on Eloise's finger, then do the same for the Modern Groom's ring."

Devlin shooed Noah and me outside.

"It's freezing out here," Noah said.

I made faces at Devlin to hurry up.

Finally, he waved us in.

"Back outside, please," Devlin said. "You didn't look thrilled enough when you came in."

Oh, God.

Fifteen minutes later, my toes frostbitten and Noah's ears bright red, Devlin was satisfied with our fake expressions.

"Modern Bride," said Devlin, "beam with delight as you pick up your wedding ring and slowly slide it on your—"

"Eloise," Astrid interrupted, "move your engagement ring to your right hand."

I pulled off the diamond ring—for the first time since Noah slid it on—and was flooded with relief.

Whoa.

I slid it back on.

Instant panic. A call for Tums.

Oh, God. Oh, God. Oh, God.

"Eloise, your *other* right hand," Devlin said with a snort.

I took off the ring—again, blissful relief—and slid it on

the fourth finger of my right hand. Where it didn't be-
long. The relief remained.

I glanced at Noah, who was politely half smiling as he
awaited his big photographic moment. Polite, supportive
Noah, who'd come home early from his business trip just
to be there when I got home. Wonderful, sweet, kind,
good-looking Noah, who was edging toward being five
minutes late for a press conference Robert De Niro was
holding in Tribeca.

"Eloise, *put* on the wedding ring, please," Devlin
scolded. "We've got to finish up. The Classic Bride's shoot
at Circle of Love jewelers is set for four."

Philippa's wedding ring would be gorgeous. A beautiful, simple, classic gold band, perhaps accented by baguettes. She got a circle of love; I got scrap metal.

"Eloise…" Devlin muttered.

Noah tapped me on the nose.

I hadn't realized I was staring into space. I slid on the
wedding ring, waiting for my stomach to roll, waiting for
the panic, Tums at the ready in my pocket.

Turned out the ring was so ridiculous that it didn't
bother me one bit.

I was on my way home from Round Rings (Noah
had sped off to the press conference) when Jane called
from one of those huge stores in which everything
costs under ten dollars. She'd been searching every shoe
shop and department store for red, white and blue
shoes for her bridal party, when she passed the dollar
store and spied in the window a pair of white pleather
pumps with a tiny American flag on the heel. Price:
$4.99. She wanted to hold a mini Flirt Night Round
Table for our opinions on whether or not Ina would

consider super-ridiculous bargain-bin shoes a hostile gesture.

Over hot chocolates and s'mores (complete with a lit candle to melt the marshmallows between the graham crackers and the chocolate bar. Yum!) in DT★UT, our favorite coffee lounge, Amanda and I (Natasha and Summer were visiting Grandma and Grandpa) advised Jane to tell Ina that she'd found them on sale in Bloomingdale's.

Amanda stuck her marshmallow in the little fire. "Tell Ina the salesman said if you bought them any closer to July Fourth, they'd be two hundred bucks."

Jane pulled one of the shoes out of the huge plastic shopping bag (the shoes didn't even come in boxes) and placed it on our table. "She won't know this cost $4.99 from a dollar store?"

"Trust me," I assured her. "Only our feet will know the difference."

Jane and Amanda laughed, and we built our s'mores.

"You're sure they're not too ridiculous?" Jane asked, eyeing the tiny flag on the heel.

"They're almost cute," I said. "Though the flag's missing around forty-five stars."

Amanda smiled. "Besides, what are bridesmaids for? For torturing, that's what. Aren't we proving that by wearing rubber dresses at Eloise's wedding?"

"Just think," Jane said, sipping her hot chocolate. "When these shoes are on your feet, I'll be *married*. Isn't that wild? Eloise, you'll already be married for *months* at my wedding."

"You novices," Amanda said. "I'm an old married woman."

For the past twenty minutes, I'd been on ring-twist alert, and neither Jane nor Amanda had even touched their rings. Meanwhile, every time I looked down at my ring, my right hand was on it, tugging away.

I ate the last crumb of my s'more. "Okay, Flirt Night Round Table Discussion 1,000,002—how do you know?"

"How do we know what?" Jane asked.

"That your guys are *it?* That Ethan and Jeff are the one? How do you know?"

Amanda leaned close. "Don't kill me for saying this. But it's just like they tell you—you just *know.*"

"But what does that really *mean?*" I asked. "I need specifics."

"It means you know you're home," Jane said, tucking her brown hair behind her ear. "It means he *is* home. He feels like your family. You feel absolutely comfortable. You know you'll get the truth, but with support. You know you'll argue, but that you'll both be there the next morning. It means love."

"And jackass in-laws," Amanda put in.

"Hear, hear," I agreed. "That I *do* know."

"I really like Ethan's family," Jane said.

"Yeah, because they're in Texas," Amanda pointed out.

"Jeff's family is in Louisiana," I reminded her.

Amanda groaned. "They might as well be at the next table."

"Eloise, are you having doubts again?" Jane asked.

Yes. No. Yes. No. Yes. No.

I don't know.

I groaned again. "One day I'm so sure that he's it, the absolute one, and I'm so happy about getting married. And then I get the heartburning doubts."

"Cold feet," Jane said.

"Jitters," Amanda offered.

"But how do I know they're not *more* than that?" I asked. "How do I know I don't have a case of 'Your body is trying to tell you *not* to marry this guy. He's *not* the one. *Run!*'"

Jane laughed. "Because Noah *is* the one."

"How do you know?"

"Because I've never seen you like this, Eloise," Jane said. "I've known you for eight years, and I've never seen you so yourself."

"Myself? What are you talking about? I've never felt so *not* myself."

"I know what she means, Eloise," Amanda said. "And I think I know what you mean, too. Noah's changed you. You do love him and he is the one, so you've been forced to—I don't know, deal with stuff, lose the defense mechanisms, that kind of thing. You've dated all these guys who couldn't possibly be the one. And then you met Noah and he fit like a glove, and all your defense mechanisms went blickety-black."

"Blickety-black?" I asked.

"Kapooey," Jane defined.

Amanda whipped her long blond hair forward over one shoulder and braided it, then whipped it back. "Case in point, Eloise—you met Noah, and two years later you're looking for your father—with your brother, no less."

"Before you were engaged, we didn't even know about your father," Jane said gently.

"Now, you're the you-est you've ever been," Amanda said. "No, you're on your way to being your you-est. It's like you've been blown wide open."

"Great, so Noah's blown me wide open. When he leaves, I'll be like Humpty Dumpty—all the king's horses and all the king's men won't be able to put me back together again."

"You're not broken, Eloise," Jane said. She wasn't one to mix metaphors. "Broken and blown wide open are two very different things. Broken, bad and sad. Open, good and gooder. And besides, where's Noah going?"

"When it's over," I clarified.

"When what's over?" Amanda asked.

"Us, me and Noah."

"Eloise, why would it ever be over?" Jane asked. "You're getting married."

"Do you think there's a class at the Learn It Center in remedial relationships?" I asked. "I'd like to sign up for a double session."

Jane laughed. "I'm not saying life comes with guarantees, Eloise. God knows, we both know it doesn't. But just because 'this and that' doesn't mean Noah's going to just walk out on you one day."

Then why do I check the closet every morning to make sure his at-the-ready bag is still there instead of a note? And when he's away on a trip, why do I look at the spot where the bag should be and cry and worry that he won't come home?

"Because you're scared out of your mind about losing him," Jane said.

I stared up at her.

Jane squeezed my hand. "No, you didn't say it aloud, but I know what you were thinking."

It was what I was always thinking.

I kissed her hand. "Why can't I just marry you?"

Jane and Amanda laughed.

"To lesbians," Amanda said, holding up her mug. "They get to marry the women they love—well, in some places, anyway."

We clinked.

* * *

In addition to my and Philippa's *Why I Said Yes!* columns, Astrid was running two additional *Why I Said Yes!*
pieces so that readers wouldn't feel cheated of their regular monthly features. According to Astrid's warped view,
because Philippa and I were getting free dream weddings,
readers would consider us on a par with celebrities; therefore, she still wanted the "common bride's" perspective for
her "common readership."

One of the "common bride's" columns was in my in-
box for an accompanying graphic. It was so stupid and offensive that I understood immediately why Astrid had
chosen it. "Provocative points of view ensure that our
readers will rant and rave to their friends, to online wed-
ding-discussion groups and in letters to the magazine," Astrid had announced a hundred times when a staffer ranted
and raved about how offensive an article or column was.
"It's instant publicity. It gets *Wow* on daytime talk shows."

I wouldn't be surprised to find Astrid and June's common bride, Julie G., twenty-seven, of Atlanta, Georgia, on
The View, defending her misguided perspective. In one
thousand wasted words, Julie described how she had said
yes because she'd finally reached her goal of losing eleven
pounds (eleven instead of ten just so she'd be able to
enjoy a single M&M without panicking) and was now, at
five feet six inches tall, a svelte size four and one hundred
ten pounds.

*"And I owe it all to Jim. Thanks to him gently calling me
Tubby and wagging his finger when I reached for the cookie jar
and letting me know in no uncertain terms that no weight loss
equaled no marriage proposal, I'm now going to be Mrs. Skinny
Bride!"*

That was a direct quote, I kid you not. And it would

jump out, literally, because it was exactly the quote Astrid wanted highlighted for bolded quote that captured the spirit of the column.

Instead of designing a graphic to accompany Mrs. Skinny Bride's column, I clicked on Word and typed *Why I Said Yes! by Eloise Manfred.*

I said yes because Noah is home. Figuratively speaking, of course.

And that was true. Noah *was* home. He *did* feel like family. I *was* completely comfortable. But, argument or no argument, I *didn't* know that Noah would be there in the morning.

Which was the problem. Noah *wasn't* home. In the literal sense.

"Eloise, did you ever stop to think that you chose Noah *because* he's never home?" Jane had asked last night at the coffee lounge.

"I chose him because he's not home?" I repeated. "Huh?"

Jane had leaned forward. "Eloise, you chose a guy who travels for business every weekend and at least once during the week. You chose a guy who's around a few days a week."

"I *chose?*" I repeated again. "Like I knew he was Mr. Jet Plane when I met him?"

"You yourself said you liked Noah so much immediately that you threw up during your first date," Amanda put in.

"And then the less he was around," Jane said, "the more comfortable you were."

"That's ridic—" True, I amended.

During our first date, when I excused myself to the ladies' room to refresh my lipstick and catch my breath and assure myself that you couldn't possibly fall in love with a guy you'd known for an hour and a half, I looked at myself in the mirror and smiled like an idiot and threw up.

When I returned to the table, Noah had ordered a surprise dessert and another round of margaritas, and he told me that I looked absolutely beautiful.

But I just barfed my brains out in the bathroom, I thought. *And now I'll have to go back because you're even more perfect than you were when I threw up the first time.*

Turned out I didn't have to, because over fried ice cream and mango margaritas, Noah told me that he couldn't wait to go out with me again but that he'd have to because he was going away for the next two weekends. "I travel a lot," he'd told me. "Constantly, really."

My nausea disappeared.

The less he was around, the more comfortable you got...

Until he proposed.

Get back to work, I yelled at myself.

For Julie G.'s graphic, I decided on a balding, potbellied cartoon man wagging a finger at an emaciated woman in lingerie, a thought-bubble over his head that said: "No sex for you until you lose that one pound! I saw you sneak that M&M, you Tubby!"

Today's Modern Bride couldn't get fired, could she?

chapter 14

The moment I let Astrid know that Emmett was interested, after all, in being the "young, hip father" for the Grooms-and-Fathers-To-Be feature, she buzzed her assistant.

"Carol, call Perfect People and cancel the young, hip male for tomorrow's G&F To-Be shoot." She glanced up at me. "Gold star, Eloise."

Three days later, Emmett arrived on time at the studio. Astrid and Devlin looked him up and down, down and up, and nodded.

"Perfection," Astrid said, taking in his faded The Cure T-shirt, black leather jacket and huge black boots. "Gold star, Eloise."

"Is she for real?" Emmett whispered.

"'Fraid so," I said.

"If I could just add a tiny drop of hair gel," Devlin said, squeezing a tube of Dippity-Do at Emmett.

"No way," Emmett protested, holding up his hands.

"Devlin, please don't upset the talent," Astrid intervened.

"Fine, whatever," Devlin muttered. "I won't upset the talent."

"Waaah. Waah! Waaaaaaaaaah!"

"What is that earsplitting noise?" Emmett asked. "It sounds like someone stepped on a seal."

"It's a *baby.*"

We whirled around. Coming toward us with a baby in a Baby Bjorn strapped to her chest was Brianna Harris, *Wow*'s cranky managing editor.

I kissed her on the cheek and oohed and aahed over the baby, who was beautiful but loud. "Brianna, I thought you were still on maternity leave!"

"Yeah, me too," she muttered in my ear. "But Astrid insisted I drag in the baby for a shoot. She said she was desperate for an infant because a real-lifer backed out of a shoot at the last minute."

Who was I to tell her that the last minute was actually last week, and Astrid just wanted to save money. Infant models weren't cheap. Except when they were free. Translation: the newborn of your terrified-of-you employee.

"The talent should practice holding the baby," Devlin said to Emmett.

"The talent has a name," Emmett snapped.

"The talent has an attitude," Devlin whispered loudly.

"The talent is a *teenager,*" Brianna said, eyeing Emmett. "No way is he holding Caitlin."

"I happen to be twenty-nine," Emmett said.

"Have you ever held a baby?" Brianna asked.

"I've held a puppy," he told her.

"Oh, that's really the same," she muttered.

"Brianna, since you were kind enough to come in on your maternity leave, why don't you show Emmett how to hold the baby," Astrid suggested. She had her *as my second in command, I would think you could have thought of that yourself* expression.

Hey, guess what, Astrid, Brianna shouldn't even be here!

"You have to be really careful," Brianna told Emmett, taking tiny Caitlin out of the Baby Bjorn, which hardly seemed possible to do yourself. "If you don't support her neck, you'll break it."

Emmett backed away.

Uh-oh. When Emmett had turned up this morning, on time, no less, I'd sneaked away for a moment to call Charla and let her know that Emmett hadn't freaked out on the way. She was sure that the moment Emmett laid eyes on a baby, a sweet, baby-powder-smelling, cooing, gurgling baby, he would either turn to mush or turn to the nearest airport for a one-way ticket to Anywhere Else.

At this rate, it was Destination Airport.

"It's okay, Emmett," I told him. "You just slip your hand under her neck, like this—" I took the baby from Brianna. "And another hand under her bottom. And she'll be just fine. Won't you, little baby girl?"

"How do you know how to do that?" he asked.

"Friend of mine has a baby," I told him. "Just takes doing it a few times and then you feel totally comfortable."

"I don't know," Emmett said. "I thought I could do this, but— Can't I hold a baby doll?"

"Baby dolls tend to look like *baby dolls* in photographs," Devlin pointed out with a *did this guy graduate from elementary school?* expression.

I glared at Devlin. "Ready?" I asked Emmett.

He stared at the baby, her big blue trusting eyes staring back. "Uh, I guess so."

"Guessing so isn't good enough," Brianna yelped. "You're either ready or you're not."

Emmett looked to me for help. "I don't know."

"Five hundred bucks," I singsonged in his ear.

"I'm ready," he said. "Tell me when to start smiling. I just slip my hand under her neck…" He did so, carefully, practically biting his lower lip. "And then I slip this hand under her bottom."

Voilà, he was holding the baby.

Baby Caitlin's little rosy-red mouth twitched, and Emmett's entire expression changed. His eyes widened, his features relaxed and he smiled.

"She smells good," he said. "I expected her to smell like—"

"Shit?" I asked.

He laughed. "Yeah. But she smells like baby powder. Hi, baby," he cooed.

"You can sway a little, back and forth," Brianna said. "Babies really like that."

Emmett swayed. The rosy-red mouth twitched.

"She's so light," Emmett whispered. "She weights next to nothing."

"Eleven pounds, to be exact," Brianna said.

Emmett touched a finger to Caitlin's face. "Is it okay if I touch her face?" he asked Brianna.

"You get points for asking," Brianna said. "But you really shouldn't, not until she's had her immunizations."

"Babies are pretty delicate," I said.

"I can't touch you until you've had your shots," Emmett whispered to Caitlin. "Otherwise, I would give you a little kiss on your nose."

Okay, where did my brother go? And who was this mad impostor?

I couldn't wait to call Charla.

"I can't believe I'm really holding a baby," Emmett cooed to Caitlin.

"Okay, people, that's a wrap," Devlin said, putting away his camera.

Startled, Emmett and I both glanced at Devlin. He was putting away his equipment.

"But Devlin, we didn't even start yet," I said.

"Are you kidding? I shot six rolls of film," Devlin responded. "The talent's got talent, after all. He's a natural at modeling—and at fatherhood too."

"I'm not a model," Emmett growled.

I waited for him to add, *Or a father.*

But he didn't.

I sneaked off to call Charla.

The next day, Devlin dropped off the proofs from Emmett's shoot. "Tell your brother to sign with an agency," he said, tossing the folder onto my desk. "When the June issue comes out, everyone's going to want him."

"Emmett's sort of antimodeling," I explained.

"Yeah, that's why I have six rolls of him modeling," Devlin snorted. "Trust me, I know the type. Mr. Antiestablishment until the Establishment calls and offers a boatload of money."

"Sometimes it's not a matter of principle—it's a matter of necessity," I said, surprised I was defending Emmett.

"Well, whatever you want to call it, it's worth a lot of money. He's got it."

"Thanks. I'll let him know."

Devlin finally clicked down the hall, and I slid out the

contact sheet. Three of the shots were blown up, eight and a half by eleven. One in black and white and two in color.

Was Emmett really this good-looking? I knew he was, but he really did *look* like a model in the photos, like a professional, million-dollar-an-hour model. He was all angles and too-cool-for-words, but dimpled and sweet.

In my favorite of the three, he held little Caitlin so carefully, the pink swaddling blanket at such contrast with Emmett's rock-concert T-shirt and black leather jacket. The baby slept peacefully while Rebel Who Now Had A Cause To Stop Rebelling held her against his chest.

After work, I took the subway downtown to Charla's apartment to drop off the photos. Charla hadn't called last night to marvel at what a changed man Emmett was from the photo shoot, which might mean he went from awestruck to dumbstruck and stayed there. The photos just might bring him back to awestruck.

Emmett wasn't home, but Charla was. She was watching a prenatal yoga tape and contorting herself into strange positions on the living-room floor. While she let out an occasional "om," I sat on the sofa and leafed through the magazine on the coffee table. It was *Power Pregnancy,* one of the magazines owned by *Wow*'s parent company.

I flipped through it. *What's Going On Inside Your Womb Today? How To Hire a Nanny. How To Feel Sexy When You're Due Any Day!* And a quiz, "Are You Really Ready For Parenthood?", which Charla had taken.

She'd scored twelve out of a hundred. That couldn't be good.

Score: 0–12: Parenthood is more than chromosomes. Here's a list of some excellent books, Web sites and government and community resources to educate you about parenthood....

"Charla?"

No answer.

"Charla, don't worry about this stupid quiz, okay?"

No answer. Her palms were on her knees and her eyes were closed.

"Charla, these quizzes are written by temps who have no idea what they're talking about. They're as meaningful as horoscopes. Trust me, I—"

"Huh?" she asked. "I didn't take that qui—" She raced to the couch and grabbed the magazine. "Oh no!"

"Emmett?"

She nodded.

Question 3: *Your baby has diaper rash. You:*

A)   *Apply ointment to baby's bottom*

B)   *Apply ointment to the diaper—after all, it's* diaper *rash.*

C)   *Rash? Ewwww!*

Emmett circled B *and* C.

Charla groaned. "No wonder he was so quiet this morning and then suddenly wanted to take a long walk. How much do you want to bet that Emmett will call and say he's staying at a friend's tonight?"

"A lifetime supply of Pampers?"

"And Desitin," she added before dropping down on the sofa with a sigh.

"It's just a stupid quiz," I said.

But I had no doubt that it had scared Emmett right back into his shell.

"Look at these," I told her, sliding out the photos. "He might not be ready for parenthood in terms of knowing which end of a diaper is up, but he's ready in other ways."

She looked at the photos and tears came to her eyes. "I'm not even sure he should see these. Now that he's so freaked about his parenting know-how, the reality of himself with a newborn might really send him to some mountain."

"Ah, but you can learn where diaper rash ointment goes, but you can't learn to make that expression."

She smiled and traced over the photo with her finger. "Maybe he was able to be so touched because it's not his kid."

I squeezed her hand. "Or maybe he'll be even more awestruck when it is."

chapter 15

According to Noah, a guy couldn't fake the look on Emmett's face in the photographs.

"It's the exact opposite of the look on my face right now," he whispered to me, moving a bite of we-weren't-sure-what in his mouth. "And trust me, I'm trying to be polite. *What* am I eating?"

We were in the sampling room at Yum's, a new catering house that specialized in meeting "the unique dietary needs of today's world." They'd paid big bucks to be included in the wedding feature.

"Prime rib?" I answered, but I wasn't sure. The small pieces of food on our little plastic plates looked like prime rib. From the color, to the shape, to the texture, to the rim of fat along the side. But it didn't quite taste like prime rib.

"Mmm," Astrid said. She took one of the tiny cups on a silver platter to "cleanse her palate." "Simply delicious. Very light, yet still substantial."

"That's a hallmark of Prime Fib," the manager of Yum's said.

"Prime *Fib?*" I asked. "Like prime rib but it's a fib because it's not, um, real meat?"

"Exactly!" said the woman.

"This is tofu?" Noah asked, no longer chewing—or swallowing. I saw him glancing around discreetly for a garbage can or a dog.

"It's seitan," the manager said. "Isn't it simply delicious?"

Ask Mini-Astrid. From the pre-vomit look on her face, I would say *no.*

"Um, is there a choice of fish or chicken as well?" Noah asked.

Please say yes. Please say yes. Please say yes.

"Scandalous!" said the manager. "Don't even use those words on these premises!" She smiled. "We're strictly vegetarian."

"But *we're* not," I said, wagging a finger between Noah and me.

"Ah, but the Modern Bride *is,*" was Astrid's contribution.

"Philippa's a vegetarian, and she's the Classic Bride," I pointed out.

I could only imagine the delectable prime rib or filet mignon or chicken cordon bleu that would be heaped on her plate at her wedding.

"We'll be offering a choice of Prime Fib," the manager announced. "And Soydfish."

"Soydfish?" Noah repeated.

"Looks and tastes *almost* like swordfish," she explained. "But it's soy, soy and more soy! Sides will be our famous asparagus in ginger sauce and curried sweet potatoes."

I wanted to wail like Caitlin. Waaah!

"Why don't you two move on to our sipping station?" the manager said, gesturing us toward a counter with some Dixie cups and bottles of seltzer. "Our Soydfish samples will be ready in moments."

"Eloise, can't you talk to your boss?" Noah whispered in my ear as he downed five cups of seltzer. He didn't even like seltzer. "Just explain that no one you know is a vegetarian, and therefore no one at your wedding will be a vegetarian. Unless, of course, the guest list will be manufactured also."

Gulp. It actually would be. Not all of it, but in my inbox yesterday I found a press release about the Today's Bride feature. Noted invitees to the Modern Bride's wedding were Lenny Kravitz, Pink, the *Queer Eye for the Straight Guy* team, Cameron Diaz and the Hilton sisters. One noted invitee to the Classic Bride's wedding was the queen of England.

Note the word *invitees* and not *guests.* Astrid was hoping that no one would note it, of course. The celebs and dignitaries would be invited for name dropping in the feature, but *Wow* and its advertisers didn't expect them to come.

"Eloise?" Noah whispered. "We *do* get to invite our friends and family to our wedding, right?"

I quickly stuffed my mouth with another piece of Prime Fib. "It sort of tastes just like chicken!" I told Noah with a hopeful expression.

He shook his head at me. "It sort of tastes just like shit."

"I got an F on my wedding-planning diary for the caterer visit," Philippa said as we rode the elevator down and away from another day at *Wow.* "Astrid had Mini-Astrid rewrite it for me. I totally hurled when I read the 'new and improved version.'"

"Can I see the original?" I asked.

She pulled it out of her tote bag and uncrumpled it.

"Astrid crumpled it into a ball?" I asked. Not that I would put it past Acid, but I was still surprised.

"No, I did," Philippa said. "You'll see why."

Dear Wedding Diary, All the guests at my wedding are going to be stricken with mad cow disease.

She went on to describe what went on at slaughter-houses, how the grain used to feed cows could feed starving children instead and ended with the statement that animals were people too.

Actually, they're not, Astrid scrawled in red in the margin. *They're animals.*

"*She's* an animal!" Philippa seethed. "No, I take that back. Animals are wonderful. Astrid is…the scummy stuff you have to scrape off your shower walls."

I laughed. "No, she's the dog poop you step into on the street and then can't get out of the grooves of your sneakers!"

She howled. And for the next minutes we played "Astrid is…" one-ups and both felt much better.

"Hey, what did you get on your diary?" she asked.

"An F minus," I said. "Mini-Astrid is rewriting it for me as we speak. Astrid didn't appreciate my tofu jokes."

"Good job!" she said and high-fived me.

"So how are things going with your parents and brother?" I asked.

"Same. They hate me," she said.

Whoever she was, Phyllis Wilschitz or Philippa Wills, *I* liked her.

I knew one person who'd enjoy dinner at my wedding: Charla Gould. For someone who ate three hamburgers in four hours last Saturday, she was now wolfing down a soy salami sandwich as though it were…meat.

Charla, Natasha, Summer and I were at an indoor playground filled with squealing, running toddlers and crawling infants and their mothers and caregivers. A minute ago, Summer had declared it snack time and went running for her stroller and its hanging diaper bag, which was always filled with treats and her sippy cup of juice.

Summer pawed at the bag. "Cookie!"

"After a healthy snack, sweetie," Natasha told her, tapping Summer on the nose. "What does Mommy have for Summer in here?" She reached in and pulled out a banana. "Yummy! Banana!"

Summer eyed the banana, then ran to Charla and stared at her sandwich. "Me," she said, pointing.

Charla ripped off a little piece and offered it to Summer. The toddler stared at it, then took it, slowly put it in her mouth, made a face, pulled it out and dropped it in Natasha's palm. "Bana. Bana!" she said, running back to her mother.

We laughed.

"I've been craving salami like mad," Charla said. "But the nitrates aren't good for the baby. I swear this stuff tastes just like the real thing! Taste this," she offered, handing over her sandwich. "You can't even tell it's not real salami. Soy is amazing."

"Oy," Summer said, running circles around Charla, her banana in hand. "Oy!"

I took a bite. Oy was right. What Charla had placed inside her pita didn't taste anything like salami.

"Wow, that's going to be me soon," Charla said, eyeing a very pregnant woman who was watching her toddler climb a mini-obstacle course. She turned to Natasha. "Does it hurt?"

"To be that pregnant?" Natasha asked. "No. Well, sometimes it's a little uncomfortable. Sometimes a lot uncomfortable. But it doesn't ever hurt."

"Until D-day," Charla said. "Right?"

"That hurts," Natasha agreed. "But it's worth it."

"So, were you—" Charla began, then shook her head and looked away.

Natasha squeezed Charla's hand. "It's okay, Charla. You can ask me anything."

That, in fact, was the reason we were all here. Charla was full of questions about pregnancy and delivery and parenthood, but she didn't know any pregnant women or new mothers. And so I'd arranged a blind date of sorts for her and Natasha.

"Omigod! You're Natasha Nutley!" said a mother whose infant was crawling to the ball in Summer's hands.

"Shh." Natasha smiled and put a finger to her lips. "I'm trying to keep a low profile."

"Ooh, sorry," the woman said. "I love *All My Children!* This is so exciting! Will you autograph this?" she asked, taking a burp cloth off her shoulder.

Natasha laughed. "I'd love to." She signed her name on the white cloth. The woman scooped up her autograph and baby, all smiles.

"This is going to sound really dumb," Charla began. "But it's almost weird to think that even famous TV stars have babies. I mean, there you were, in the delivery room, screaming your head off like everyone else, right?"

Natasha smiled. "Some stuff you can't pay someone else to do for you."

"And our friend Jane was there to prove it," I put in.

"You can have a friend with you in the delivery room?"

Charla asked. "I thought only the doctors and nurses and the baby's father."

"You can have anyone, really," Natasha said. "With me were my OB, a couple of nurses, Jane, my aunt and my mother. It's amazing—my entire life, my mother and I have never gotten along, not even through the pregnancy. I was resigned to her and my father not being in my child's life."

Charla bit her lip. "That must have been so hard."

"It was," Natasha confirmed. "Without Summer's father's support and my parents' support, I really had to fend for myself during my pregnancy. But I learned who my friends are—" she smiled at me "—and I learned that I'm a really strong person. I feel like I can do anything."

"But you and your mom reconciled?" Charla asked.

Natasha nodded. "At the eleventh hour. My aunt was my Lamaze coach, and when I went into labor, she called my mom, and I guess my twelve hours of labor gave her time to think that she wanted to be there when my baby was born. She and my father were waiting in the hospital when my aunt and I arrived."

"I'm glad," Charla said. "Sure would be nice if Emmett would be there."

"What do you think the chances are?" Natasha asked.

Charla stared at her feet. "Slim to none. He's been staying with his grandmother for the past few days. He said she was feeling under the weather, and wanted to help her out."

My grandmother was feeling absolutely fine.

"Did you talk to him about the parenthood quiz in *Power Pregnancy?*" I asked Charla.

"I tried, but he wouldn't even let me finish the sentence. He said he was just fooling around and didn't even answer the questions honestly, but I saw that he did."

"How low did he score?" Natasha asked.

"He got a twelve out of a hundred," Charla said. "Which added up to—*No, Babies* Can't *Take a Sleeping Pill.*"

We laughed, but Charla sobered up fast. "I'm so afraid he's going to walk out on me. On us," she added, patting her belly.

"He's probably just sorting things out," Natasha said. "Letting it all sink in. It means changing his entire life. He's probably just going through the pain of adjustment."

Charla cheered up a bit. "Does that sound about right to you, Eloise? You know him best."

That might have been true once, but now I didn't know Emmett at all.

That, however, wasn't going to help Charla.

"Emmett's always managed to surprise me," I said. Which was true.

"Omigod," exclaimed another of the mothers. "Are you Natasha Nutley? From *All My Children?*"

Natasha smiled. "I am. And this little cherub is my daughter."

"Omigod!" the woman shrieked again. "Haley," she said to her toddler, "you're playing with the daughter of a famous soap opera actress!"

Hayley couldn't care less. "Da-da!" she said, pointing at a man trying to disengage a little boy from the top of the slide. "Da-da!"

"Da-da," Summer repeated.

The woman bent down next to Summer. "That's Hayley's daddy, but I'll bet you're going to see your daddy at home later."

"Da-da," Summer said.

"Her father lives in California," Natasha told the woman.

"How nice—I'll bet you visit your daddy often."

No, actually I don't.

Why not?

Because he's not i-n-t-e-r-e-s-t-e-d in knowing me.

"Summer, sweetheart, let's go swing!" Natasha said. The woman's cheeks flushed.

Summer went running, a big smile on her beautiful face.

Charla pulled her cell phone out of her purse and punched in some numbers. "Emmett, it's Charla. If I don't hear from you today, I will be on a plane to Oregon tomorrow to live with my mom. I'd rather my baby had a close grandmother than an absentee father. Wow—Emmett, I guess this really could be a repeat of your own life. The life you're so pissed about. The life you're running away from. Nice thing to do to an innocent kid, huh?" Click. She turned to me. "The cycle needs to end with him."

I nodded, too impressed to speak.

chapter 16

I waited until ten the next morning for my phone to ring. It didn't.

Was Charla on her way to the airport? Was Emmett drinking himself into oblivion in some bar? Was I going to Pennsylvania alone today?

Uh, hello, Theodore Leo Manfred, I'm the daughter you abandoned like a paper towel twenty-seven years ago. My brother didn't come with me today because he's too busy abandoning his own girlfriend and baby. You know what they say about the apple and the tree...

Directions to Boonsonville, Pennsylvania, in hand, I stepped out of the elevator into the lobby of my apartment building and burst into tears.

"Eloise, dear?" asked an elderly neighbor. "Are you all right? Why don't you sit down and take a deep breath."

I sat. I breathed.

I stared at my watch. I'd left a message for Emmett earlier in the week to let him know I was leaving at 10:00 a.m. sharp on Saturday morning.

Was he really not coming? Was he really letting Charla go?

I will not stall. I will not sit here for ten minutes and then fifteen minutes and then a half hour and then suddenly it's noon and he's still not here but I am.

Go.

You can stall for an extra few minutes by checking to see if the mail arrived, I realized. After all, Emmett would be coming from Grams's apartment, and perhaps she'd asked him to help her out with something. Or maybe he was on his way but stopped to pick up bagels and coffee for the road. Maybe—

Maybe the invitation to my wedding was in my mailbox.

I ignored the catalogs, the bills, the junk mail.

I pulled out the heart-shaped red envelope.

It was addressed to *Eloise Manfred and Guest.*

Great! I got to bring a date!

Thank God Noah had left for London (some scandal involving Madonna and her husband) at the crack of dawn and hadn't seen this. Eloise Manfred and *Guest?*

I slit open the envelope. A yellow sticky note covered the invitation, which, by the way, was magnetized so that you could put it on your refrigerator.

Eloise: Please proof the copy and return to the production editor with any changes or corrections by Monday at noon. —AO

Eyes closed, I slowly peeled off the sticky note. Stamped in black type on a red leather heart was:

Eloise Manfred and Groom's Name Here
Invite You To Their
Pairing Union
at Fifth Avenue Fantasy
February Twenty-Ninth @ 10:00 p.m.

* * *

I wasn't getting married. I was being paired. I was having a pairing union.

And till when? Four a.m.? What wedding—pairing union—began at 10:00 p.m.?

The cutting of the cake would probably be at 2:00 a.m.

If I was even having a cake. That sounded mighty traditional.

Instead of a cake, I would probably be having wedding pumpkin seeds or Jell-O. Yellow Jell-O. Soy, tofu, seitan yellow Jell-O. With my guests Lenny Kravitz and Mini-Astrid and the proprietor of Round Rings.

Whose wedding is it anyway?

Not mine, that was for sure.

I sank back down in the lobby chair, completely exhausted at 10:17 a.m.

"Yay, she's still here!"

I turned around to find Charla, her pigtails wound around the side of her head like Princess Leia, all smiles. Standing next to her, hands in his pocket, was Emmett.

For the first hour on the road, I was the cranky one. One-word answers. A few "But you just went to the bathroom a half hour ago, Charla!" Several snaps at Emmett for the too-loud volume on his Walkman. Twice, I even told my growling stomach to shut the hell up.

"Eloise, are you all right?" Charla asked.

"I just have a lot on my mind," I said.

Selfish! I yelled at myself. *You have a lot on your mind? You're marrying a great guy at a free wedding—a freak's wedding, but a free wedding. Charla's pregnant by the most immature man alive and Emmett needs attention. Serious attention. Stop being so self-absorbed, Eloise!*

Ah, I felt much better. Nothing like a little self-scolding to get yourself out of the doldrums.

"Charla, do you need to use the rest room?" I asked. "There's one coming up in two miles."

"No, I'm okay," she said.

"Emmett, are you hungry?"

I peered at him in the rearview mirror. He shook his head without looking up.

We drove in silence until we reached the Pennsylvania border. Emmett sat up at the sign and stared gloomily out the window. Charla alternated between staring at his profile and reading *What To Expect When You're Expecting*. She'd tried reading aloud, but Emmett said it was way too early to hear the word *umbilical cord*.

Boonsonville, this exit.

As I passed the sign, my heart started pounding. *I'm here. I'm in the town where my father lives.*

Might live, I amended.

Which allowed me to keep driving. Slowly. It was one thing to drive endlessly. It was another to get to where you were going.

"We're here," I said, my stomach flip-flopping.

"We're where?" Emmett asked, looking out the window. "We're nowhere."

"I mean, we just got off our exit. We're in Boonsonville."

Boom. Boom. Boom. My forehead broke out in a sweat. *I can't do this. I can't do this. I can't do this.*

Charla held the directions. "Okay, this right should be Boonsonville Lane."

I stopped the car in the middle of the road.

"Eloise!" Charla yelped. "What are you doing! Drive! Now!"

I stepped on the gas pedal and pulled over. "I can't do it. I can't do it!"

"Let's go tell that fuckhead what we think of him," Emmett said. "We came all this way, all this bull, a lifetime of bull—we're telling him that he's the worst piece of scum on earth."

Oh, God. Oh, God. Oh, God.

"Emmett," I began. But nothing else came out of my mouth. He was entitled to feel how he felt.

Then why were we here? If he—if everyone—was entitled to his—their—feelings, then why did we judge anyone? Demand anything from anyone?

If Emmett was entitled to his feelings, why wasn't he entitled to run away from his responsibilities?

"Eloise, do you need me to drive?" Emmett asked.

"No, I'm okay." I took a deep breath. "Boonsonville Lane, here we come."

But Boonsonville Lane wasn't at the corner. Thomas Frumkin Way was.

My heart slowed down a bit.

"There are a couple of kids coming on skateboards," Charla said. "Let's ask them."

I stopped beside them and rolled down the window. The air smelled like snow.

"Excuse me," I said to the two kids. "We're looking for Boonsonville Lane."

The blond boy with the freckles nodded. "Make a right at that corner," he said, pointing. "And then go about a mile and you'll see it on the right, before the creek."

One right and one mile later, I didn't see it on my right. I did see a creek, though, which we were up without a paddle since we were clearly lost. I could hear the kids laughing from here.

"I really have to pee," Charla said. "And I'm feeling kind of—" her cheeks expanded as though she was going to throw up right on Emmett's lap "—sick."

I zoomed to the gas station we'd passed as we got off the highway. "Charla, there's a rest room," I said, pointing at a door with a tiny sign that read Out of Order. "Oops."

"It's okay," she said. "It's passed a bit. I can hold out. Why don't you ask the clerk inside where Boonsonville Lane is."

While Emmett stared moodily out the window and Charla practiced breathing, I ran inside the little store.

"Boonsonville Lane?" the clerk repeated, taking off his cap. "Boonsonville Lane. Joe," he called over his shoulder. "Is there a Boonsonville Lane around here?"

"Used to be," a man said, poking his head through the doorway. "Town council changed it."

To…

"Forget what to, though," he added.

"Well where can we find out?" I asked.

"Town council," he said. "But they're not in session. Best bet is to go to Flo's Diner and just ask. Lots of old-timers in there. One'll know."

Flo's Diner was across the street. While Charla ran for the rest room, Emmett and I slid into a booth. When the waitress came over and took a short pencil from behind her ear, I asked her if she knew which street used to be called Boonsonville Lane.

"Which street used to be called Boonsonville?" she yelled over her shoulder.

"Thomas Frumkin Way," said an elderly woman with a forkful of apple pie midway to her mouth.

Thomas Frumkin Way. So we had been there.

"Why?" asked the waitress. "You visiting relatives?"

"Old family relation," I said.

"Well, no one's lived on that street in fifteen years," the elderly woman said. "There was only a caretaker's cottage for the adjacent dairy farm, but that was razed when the horses came."

Oh.

Ask. Just ask. That's what you're here for.

I cleared my throat. "Um, did a Theo Manfred used to caretake that farm?"

Another man mock chuckled. "Theo Manfred? Caretaker? That's a laugh. He couldn't take care of *himself.*"

Emmett and I looked at each other. Emmett stared at the wall, then grabbed his jacket and ran out of the diner. I saw him spit, then lean against the car, his hands in his pockets.

"Do you know him well?" I asked the man.

He shook his head. "Not well, and not anymore. Theo lived in an apartment in the caretaker's house. Some kind of big-city writer, but he'd forget to pay his electricity and there'd be no lights, and he wouldn't even care. The caretaker would knock on the door for the rent and find him working by candlelight.

"Does he still live in town?" I asked, fighting the urge to close my eyes.

"Nah," the man replied. "He took off years ago. He said he got a newspaper job, not reporting or nothing—the job where you fix up the grammar. A small paper out in Scranton."

Scranton. "Is that far?" I asked.

"About two hours' drive north—depends on traffic, of course."

Relief flooded through me. Bring on the traffic. The farther away we were, the easier it was to keep going.

Not that there was anything easy about it. Were we supposed to drive out to Scranton and try to find a newspaper office and ask if a Theo Manfred worked there?

We didn't have a plan B. Plan A, driving to the address Noah had gotten off the Internet, had been enough.

And we'd done it. We might not have found Theo Manfred, but we found where he once lived. That was something. That was a step.

"What are you going to have, honey?" asked the waitress.

Startled, I glanced up at her. "I'm sorry, but I think my brother's not feeling well." I gestured out the window. "Thanks for everything, though." I left a ten on the table and went outside.

Emmett was leaning against the car, staring at his boots.

"If you can't deal with this, it's okay," I told him. "You don't have to do this with me. I'm ready now. You don't have to be."

He rolled his eyes. "Yeah, right. You're *forcing* me to be ready, Eloise. I'm supposed to know you're driving up and down every street in Pennsylvania looking for Asshole, and I'm just supposed to go merrily along as though nothing weird is happening."

"When did you ever go merrily along, Emmett?"

"You've been accusing me of going merrily along for years," he said. "I do whatever I want without caring about anyone or anything. Does that sound familiar?"

So he did listen.

"Look," he said. "You have a new lead. Let's just go home and you'll start fresh next weekend."

"*I'll* start fresh," I repeated.

"You just said I didn't have to come with you. That you were the one who was ready."

Yeah, but.

I want you to come with me. I need you to come with me.

Charla came out of the diner, pressing a damp paper towel against her cheeks. "Don't you know it's bad for the baby to hear arguing?"

"You're going to twist that ring right off your finger and it's going to fly out the window," Emmett said.

We were in the car, Emmett behind the wheel, I in the passenger seat, waiting for Charla, who'd decided she had a craving for cheese fries with gravy just as we'd been about to pull out of the diner's parking lot.

"Wha—" Oh. I glanced at Emmett, then down at my hand. I'd been twisting the diamond ring and hadn't realized it.

"That supposedly means you really don't want to get married," Emmett said. "Some girlfriend of mine told me that once when I wouldn't commit to her."

"You had a ring?" I asked.

"Some leather-and-plastic thing I got in Oregon," he said. "She said I started playing with it whenever she brought up commitment, and that told her I was ambivalent about her."

"Were you?"

He nodded. "Who haven't I been ambivalent about?"

"Don't you want to stop?" I asked. "Don't you want to actually love someone and not want to escape them the next day? Don't you want peace and serenity?"

He shrugged. "I have no idea what that is."

"I guess I don't either."

"So you're not sure you want to get married?" he asked.

I let out a deep breath. "I don't know. My friends say I've got commitment issues. Father issues. Abandonment issues. The works."

"But you did commit," he said, nodding at the ring. "You're getting married."

"I eat a roll of Tums a day."

"Me, too."

"Do you love Charla?" I asked.

"A little personal, don't you think?"

I rolled my eyes. "She loves you."

"Viola," he said. "Vickie. Valmont."

"Valmont isn't a girl's name, and you're not getting out of this conversation."

"Are you going to make me talk?"

"You have to grow up someday, Emmett," I said. "How about now that you've got a baby on the way?"

He stiffened. "With a sister like you, it's no wonder I gravitate toward women who don't get on my case and challenge me about my basic personality. Charla likes me the way I am. If you don't, hey, oh well."

I'd tried *Oh well* for an entire year and it hadn't worked for me. But neither did Emmett in his current form.

So should Emmett be allowed to be Emmett? Run away when he liked? Never commit? Have love pass him by because he was too emotionally immature and unwilling to do anything about it?

And news flash, Emmett: Charla does challenge you. She just understands you so well that you don't realize it.

Which meant Charla was my greatest ally at the moment.

"I'm not going to say it, Emmett, but you know what I'm thinking."

"I don't read minds, Eloise."

I rolled down the window, despite the cold air. "Our father left because he didn't want to commit. Didn't want the responsibility of a family. Didn't give a shit. That's who you want to emulate?"

"First of all, you don't know why he left," he shouted. "And second of all, Miss Judgmental, don't compare me to him. How dare you?"

The truth hurts, doesn't it?

"Why do you think he left, then?" I asked.

"Maybe he thought we'd be better off without him," he said in such a low voice I wasn't sure I'd heard him correctly.

I turned around to face him. "Emmett, is that what you're thinking? That Charla and the baby would be better off without you?"

"I'm not gonna win father of the year," he said. "I don't even have a job."

"You can get a job. You can make a million dollars an hour smiling into a camera lens. And you have a Yale degree. You can do whatever you want."

He leaned his head back and let out a deep breath. "I think about getting married, I think about a baby in a crib or a stroller, and I get totally claustrophobic. I feel like I can't breathe."

"That's how I feel about getting married," I admitted.

"So why do it?" he asked. "Maybe it's not the right time. Not the right time, not the right guy. Your gut is trying to tell you something."

"Or I'm just chickenshit, Emmett."

He glanced at me, then out the window. "Yeah, me too."

"But I think we're supposed to be," I told him. "I think that means good stuff is happening in our brains."

"Then why is the gas tank on E?" he asked, pointing at the tank indicator.

Oops.

★ ★ ★

The three of us took a vote and unanimously decided to head home. We agreed to make the trip to Scranton next weekend; Charla had even volunteered to Internet research the various city newspapers for addresses and potentially employees. Emmett and I didn't know whether to thank her or glare at her.

A half hour later, Charla announced that she had to pee yet again and had a craving for a strawberry milk shake, so we stopped at the McDonald's on the other side of the highway.

I pointed at an empty table. "Let's eat in here. I'm sick of the car. And it's beginning to smell like hamburger."

Charla wolfed down a McVeggie burger and unwrapped a fish-filet sandwich. I ate the pickles Emmett had taken off his cheeseburger; he swiped my fries when he finished his own. We slurped our shakes in companionable silence.

I slid the invitation to my wedding onto the table. "So what do you guys think of this?" I asked.

" 'Eloise Manfred and Guest'?" Emmett said. "Your fiancé could be *anyone?* If I were Noah, I'd be pissed as hell."

"He hasn't seen it," I said. "Anyway, I'm sure the 'guest' is just for the mock version. I'm sure the real envelope will be properly addressed."

" 'Properly addressed' sounds very traditional to me," Charla said with a wink.

I hoped she wasn't right.

"What's Fifth Avenue Fantasy?" Charla asked. "It sounds like a reality TV show."

"It's a company that transforms spaces into whatever you want, like a submarine or a jungle," I explained. "They own the penthouse of a midtown skyscraper and rent it out for 'ultimate fantasy' parties. They're trying to get into the wedding biz."

"So what's your fantasy wedding?" Charla asked, also swiping my fries.

Philippa's, I thought out of nowhere. *A beautiful, traditional white wedding, with flowers and real prime rib and a gown that isn't yellow. Invitations on heavy stock paper with lovely calligraphy. A ceremony and not a pairing union.*

Philippa, of course, had loved the leather invitations. A week ago, during our *Wow* trip to Invitations By Pauline, she'd run to the display case with the heart-shaped leather invitations. "Omigod, these are so cool!" she'd trilled. "I want these—ooh, I can't decide which I like better, the red or the purple."

All the *Wow Weddings* staff members in attendance had said in unison, "Does that look like a classic wedding invitation to you, Philippa?"

Philippa sighed and put the leather invitation back on the display. She turned to the table across the aisle. "Oh look, there's a really *boring* invitation. I'm sure that's the one I 'picked,' though—right?"

Astrid narrowed her eyes. "Philippa, your attitude does not reflect the attitude of Today's Classic Bride. If you cannot work on your attitude, I'd be happy to replace you with a stand-in."

Philippa beamed at the boring invitation. "The gold foil on the envelope is really lovely!"

Astrid's thin red lips curled into a smug smile. "I couldn't agree more, Philippa. That is why I selected that exact invitation for Today's Classic Bride."

The moment Astrid turned her back, Philippa stuck her finger down her throat and gagged.

"The invitations will be going out in two weeks," Astrid announced. "I'll need your final guest lists no later than Monday."

"You're not—" Philippa began to say, then clamped her mouth shut and eyed me.

Inviting yourself to our weddings, are you? I mentally finished. *Please, no!*

"You may each invite fifty people, including guests," Astrid said. "Your other guests will include advertisers and staff."

So my wedding table might be me, Noah and the caterer's ad salesman and his date—and Astrid. Not that she would deign to sit with a lowly staffer, even if said staffer *was* the bride.

"Earth to Eloise. Eloise Manfred, please come in."

Startled, I glanced up to find Charla staring at me as she sucked her strawberry milk shake. Emmett was smearing a French fry with ketchup on his hamburger wrapper.

"So, will Emmett and I be invited?" Charla asked.

I wasn't even sure *I* would be going.

Ba-dum-pa.

"Of course," I told her. "In fact, Noah is going to ask Emmett to be an usher. You guys, Grams, a few friends and a hundred strangers who footed the bill."

Emmett shook his head. "The whole thing sounds nutso. Whose wedding is it anyway?"

Good question, baby brother.

"It's just very modern," Charla offered in defense.

"And free," I added.

Emmett snorted. "There's no such thing as a free wedding. Any idiot knows that."

chapter 17

Woman #1: "He's too good-looking for you. No one at the reunion will believe he's really your boyfriend."

Woman #2: "Well, I'm not paying two hundred bucks an hour for an average Joe."

This was the conversation going on around Jane and Amanda and me in the reception area of Perfect People on Monday afternoon as two women flipped through the books of models' photographs. At least I wasn't the only one hiring a stand-in today.

One fake father to go, please.

"Eloise, check out this one," Amanda said, holding up the celebrity look-alike book to an eight-by-ten glossy of a handsome fifty-something. "Harrison Fordsley. Wow, he's a dead ringer!"

I shook my head. "Harrison Ford's too rugged for 'hip and cool.' I need someone more Pierce Brosnan. Billy Bob Thornton. Or Bruce Willis, with hair."

Amanda and Jane continued flipping. "Ta-da!" Jane held up a photo of Pierce McBrosnan.

"Not bad," I said, checking out the model, whose real name, according to the vital stats on the back of the photo, was Howie Schwineman. "But forget the look-alike book—I need a regular Joe. Someone who looks like me, just twenty-five years older."

They tilted their heads and studied me.

"Someone who looks like…this," I said, holding up a picture of Theo Manfred.

"That's your dad?" Amanda asked.

I nodded around the lump in my throat. That *was* my father. Once.

"It's like the last pictures I have of my father," Jane said, examining the wallet-size photo. "He's so young and handsome. It's hard to imagine this man as a fifty- or sixty-year-old man."

That was true. In my mind, Theo Manfred would always be twenty-something, wearing Levi's and a white button-down shirt and a skinny red tie. He would never age, get ill.

Amanda sat back down and flipped through the look-alike book. "I know who we need to find—Kevin Costnerberg. He could definitely be your dad."

I laughed. "You guys pick him. I can't bear it."

Jane peered at me. "Are you all right, Eloise? You don't have to do this, you know. You can tell your boss that your father is 'unavailable' and that you don't want to hire a stand-in. You don't have to explain anything to her."

"I know," I said. "But—"

But what? I didn't even know what the *but* was.

No, that wasn't true. I *did* know what the but was.

I wanted a father. For a picture, for a day, for an hour, I

wanted a father. I wanted my father to say all the things Philippa's fake father had said the day he'd visited the *Wow Weddings* offices.

I'd have to ask her how much extra she'd slipped him for that.

"Omigod," Amanda yelped, triumphantly holding up an eight-by-ten glossy. "Here he is—Kevin Costnerly!" She flipped over the photo and laughed. "His real name is Gunther."

I glanced at the photo. "Put him in a black suede trench, and he's my metrosexual dad."

"Let's watch *Field of Dreams* tonight to pay homage," Jane suggested.

"No—*Dances With Wolves,*" Amanda said. She stood up very straight and shouted, "I will find you! No matter what, I will find you!"

Jane laughed. "That was *Last of the Mohicans.*"

"Oh," Amanda said.

"Hey, how about *Waterworld,*" I joked, and they both shook their heads. "Okay, I've got it. *Bull Durham.*"

"Now you're talking," Jane said. "I'll bring the Jiffy Pop."

Ten minutes later, Kevin Costnerly was mine on next Monday for two hundred fifty an hour. The extra fifty was for the special instructions: hair gel, a black leather jacket and ten minutes, minimum, of a gushing-dad routine.

"Is this a tantrum?" Emmett asked, eyeing Summer, who was crying hysterically while trying to reach my chocolate Santa collection on a high shelf.

"No, honey," Charla said. "That's just wanting chocolate."

"So it gets worse?" Emmett asked.

"Oh yeah," I said. "A lot worse."

And then I remembered that we'd arranged this little baby-sitting gig to show Emmett the joys of parenthood, not some of the less manageable realities. Since we'd returned from Pennsylvania on Saturday, Emmett had been staying with Charla again. She'd been careful to keep all pregnancy magazines out of sight.

Natasha was on a date, Noah was *Hot News*ing with Call Me Ash, Jane and Ethan were taking Kickboxing for Couples at their health club and Amanda and Jeff were what she called "TTC," which I soon learned was Internet shorthand for "trying to conceive." In other words, they were having lots of sex.

And I had one cranky two-year-old, one hormonally challenged new friend and one freaked-out younger brother to contend with.

Summer was reaching an arm up to Charla and saying, "Me. Me!"

"Does she want to be picked up?" Emmett asked.

"I think she wants to touch my pigtails," Charla said, sitting down on the rug next to Summer.

Charla was right. For the next minutes, Summer examined, tried to mouth and flung the little sparkly red balls on Charla's rubber bands. "Me, me!" Summer said, pointing at the pigtails and stomping her feet. Charla complied, twisting Summer's wildly curly almost-shoulder-length red hair into pigtails, and Summer spent an additional ten minutes staring at herself in the mirror and smiling.

"So what do we do?" Emmett asked.

"About what?" I asked.

"Baby-sitting," he said.

"We're doing it."

"This is it?"

I nodded. "We play with Summer, give her dinner, give her a bath, play a little more, have milk and cookies, and off she goes to bed."

"At, like, eleven o'clock?" he asked.

I laughed. "At, like, eight."

"Da-da," Summer said, pointing at Emmett.

Emmett paled. "Why is she saying that?"

"Don't worry, Em," I told him. "She's not accusing you. Babies tend to categorize all men as 'Daddy.' It just means they know you're a man and not a woman."

He relaxed. "Oh. Where is her father, anyway?"

"Where ours is," I told him.

He looked at me, surprised, then at Summer. I could see him taking in that information. That this adorable little creature, not yet two years old, just three feet of sweetness and innocence and bursting with life, already had baggage.

Glum, Emmett watched Summer play with Hokey Pokey Elmo. While Elmo turned himself around and Summer squealed with delight, Emmett started to cry.

Charla and I stared at him for a moment. Was Emmett actually *crying?*

Charla put her arm around him. "Emmett, honey? Are you all right?"

"I'm such a fuckup," he said and then glanced at Summer. "Oh, shit, I didn't mean to curse in front of the baby."

Charla cupped his face with her hands. "Emmett, you're dealing with a lot."

"I have to go, okay?" Emmett said.

Charla closed her eyes for a moment, then said, "Okay."

And Emmett was gone.

Charla let out a deep breath. "I'll bet you anything that he doesn't come home tonight."

Unfortunately, the odds were in her favor.

★ ★ ★

Charla called at midnight with the news that Emmett hadn't come home.

"He's gone for good. I know it," she said. "Part of me wants to scream, 'Good riddance, and grow the hell up while you're gone.' But the other part, most of me, wants him too much."

I was trying to think of something comforting to say, when my apartment buzzer rang.

It was Emmett.

I ran back to the telephone. "Charla, he just showed up here. Let me talk to him, okay? I think everything's going to be all right."

"'Kay," she said in a shaky voice and hung up.

I opened the apartment door and watched Emmett trudge up the stairs. It figured he took the stairs instead of the elevator. We lived on the ninth floor, and walking up was doable if you absolutely had to (as I'd been annoyed to learn during a recent blackout), but there was an elevator for a reason.

"What am I going to do?" he asked me as he came inside, his cheeks red from the cold.

"You're going to do what you want to do, Emmett."

"Meaning?" he asked.

"Meaning, it would be really great if you wanted to be a father to your child," I said.

"No 'You should do this, you should do that'?" he asked. "That's what I expected from you."

What good is it if you don't want to? I thought.

If you didn't want to be a father, how could you *be* a father? You could do it out of a sense of duty, and you could rise to the occasion—and maybe you'd be rewarded in ways you never imagined.

I wondered if it worked liked that. If you could do something out of duty and end up happy, like in Hallmark Hall of Fame movies on television. Last night, I watched a cable-TV movie about a mean, lonely grandmother whose grown children had run from her the minute they could, and whose abandoned grandchildren were desperate for a home. She took them in out of duty and struggled against loving them, and then tried sticking them on a bus to some other relative—only to let the bus go by when it came.

Maybe it would be like that for Emmett.

Maybe he'd take one look at his baby and fall in love.

There's intrinsic motivation and extrinsic motivation, my grandmother had said. *Your father didn't seem to have either.*

"Am I like Dad?" Emmett asked in a small voice. "Is that who I'm going to be? That son of a bitch?"

"That's up to you, Em."

He looked at me and dropped his face in his hands.

"I hired a model to be my father for the photo shoot on Monday," I told him. "I thought you should know."

"That's pretty pathetic," he said. "A fake father?"

"Two weeks ago, I hired a fake brother just in case you didn't show up."

He stared at me. "Well, I did."

"Well, our father's not going to show up, is he?"

"Why don't you tell your boss to go to hell?" he asked.

"Because that's not what you do in the real world, Emmett. As much as I would like to, she's my boss. I need my job. I need to pay my rent and bills. And I really like my job. I might not like Astrid, but I like my job. You can't go around telling people, especially people who pay you, to go to hell just because you don't like them."

"I don't need a lecture," he said.

"Actually, little brother, you do."

He rolled his eyes. "Are you ever going to get off my case?"

"No."

"Great. You're going to be a lot of fun to be around."

"Someone's got to set you straight, Emmett."

"The baby's going to do that," he said, and I could tell he was surprised it had come out of his own mouth. He lay down on the sofa and stared up at the ceiling. "Can I crash here tonight?"

"You can," I told him, "but go home, Emmett. Someone's waiting for you." And with that, I went into my bedroom.

chapter 18

When I woke up the next morning, Emmett was fast asleep on the sofa. On his chest lay his wallet, open to a photo of Charla.

I wondered if Theo Manfred did that, looked at photos of my mother, of us. If he *had* any photographs of us. Then again, if you looked at photographs, you might as well be there with the people.

I glanced at Emmett, at the picture rising and falling with his every deep, sleeping breath. I wanted to stick around and be there when he woke up, but I had a feeling Emmett needed some alone time on safe ground, and I had to be at Fly With Us Travel in midtown at 9:00 a.m. sharp to meet the *Wow* crowd to "pick" a honeymoon destination.

Honeymoon. Wherever it was Noah and I were going on our honeymoon, I would be married when I arrived. I would be Eloise Benjamin—figuratively, if not literally.

As the Second Avenue bus bumped its way downtown, I stared at my ring and forced myself not to twist it.

I wondered where Noah and I would be going for the honeymoon. Jupiter? That would be modern. Or perhaps hell. That would be truly nouvelle!

When I arrived at Fly With Us Travel, the owner was handing out brochures to the *Wow*ers. Astrid, Mini-Astrid, Devlin, his assistant and Philippa were seated around a long oval conference table.

"We'd like to push two of our least-popular honeymoon packages," the tall, gaunt man said. "We and the two resorts are splitting the cost of the packages to ensure that both of our names are given equal treatment in the magazine feature."

Astrid nodded. "Of course."

"Given the country's patriotic spirit of late," the man said, "we'd like to highlight the good old U.S. of A.'s very special honeymoon locales."

What? I wasn't going to Tahiti? Venice? Iceland?

Ah. I was going to Hawaii! No problem. Noah and I, some white sand, the bluest of blue water—

The owner waved two brochures in the air. "So, without further ado, we are pleased to be offering the Orlando, Florida, four-star hotel package and the Chicago, Illinois, Culinary Bed-and-Breakfast package."

Huh? Were those honeymoon destinations? Which was the modern one and which was the classic one?

Astrid read my mind. "As our Classic Bride, Philippa will be going to the sunshine state of Florida. Eloise, our Modern Bride will be going to the famed windy city of Chicago."

I'm going to Chicago in the dead of winter on my honeymoon? Was that modern because no one in their right mind would do it?

I glanced at Philippa. She was staring into space. I waited for her to protest Florida, but she was barely blinking.

No: *But where's the this stack?*

No: *I want to go to Chicago in the dead of winter!*

No: *Can I call Parker for his thoughts?*

Instead, she looked as if she was about to cry.

"And guess what, Classic Bride?" the owner said, staring from me to Philippa until Mini-Astrid pointed at Philippa. "Two tickets to Walt Disney World are included free!"

No reaction. Not a peep. Not even the tiniest of snickers.

Ground control to Philippa. Come in, Philippa. Didn't you hear, you get to go to Walt Disney World and see Mickey Mouse and spend your honeymoon with thousands of children!

"I'm delighted," Astrid said. "We really need to go back to basics. And what is more basic than good old-fashioned Florida sunshine and Mickey Mouse!"

Ground control to Philippa Wills.

Nothing again.

If Astrid's nonsensical comments couldn't rouse even a grimace out of Philippa, something was really wrong.

"I love it," Astrid said. "I absolutely love it. Not only does the Classic Bride go back to basics, back to tradition, but the Modern Bride learns how to cook on her honeymoon. How positively post retro!"

Did that actually mean something?

"Classic Bride, you may choose from the Orlando four-star Hilton or the Orlando four-star Marriott," the owner said, handing her two brochures.

She didn't take them.

"Philippa, are you all right?" I asked.

"I'm not going to Florida," Philippa said quietly.

Ah. There was the Philippa I knew and had started to love.

Astrid glared at her. "Philippa, as the Classic Bride, you must accept the traditional honeymoon package. You may choose between—"

"I'm not going to Florida," Philippa repeated, her face, her voice expressionless. "I'm not going anywhere."

Astrid rolled her eyes. "Philippa, I've had just about enough—"

Philippa threw the brochures high in the air. One landed on Astrid's wrap. "I'm not going on my honeymoon because I'm dropping out of the magazine feature. You can find a new Classic Bride."

"Philippa, enough with the theatrics," Astrid scolded. "No one has time for this."

"I'm serious," Philippa yelped. "I'm dropping out. It's not worth the hassle. I want the wedding *I* want."

A vein moved in Astrid's temple. "Let me make myself absolutely clear, Philippa. Unless the *wedding* is off, the feature is *on*. Perhaps I need to remind you of the binding contract you signed—page six, paragraph one."

"The wedding *is* off," Philippa cried, and ran out the door.

I looked everywhere for Philippa. Two different Starbucks, a diner, the cosmetics counter at Bloomingdale's. I didn't have her cell-phone number, and got her machine twice at home.

Finally, I went to her apartment building. She lived in a fifth-floor walk-up seven blocks north of me, on the fifth floor, of course. When I buzzed her apartment, I didn't expect an answer, but I heard the shaky hello come through the intercom.

"Philippa, it's Eloise."

Buzzzzz.

I pushed through the heavy double doors and hiked up the stairs. Philippa was waiting on the top step, her blond hair in a ponytail, her blue eyes red-rimmed again. She'd changed into a T-shirt and jeans, two items of clothing I had never seen her wear.

"I was planning to move in with Parker once we got married, but now I guess I'll be living here forever." She broke down in sobs, and I took her hand and led her inside, to the futon that dominated the studio.

"The wedding is off?" I asked, reaching for the box of tissues on her nightstand and handing it to her.

She nodded.

"What happened?"

She sniffled and blew her nose. "I told Parker there was something I had to tell him before we got married and that was that."

"He called off the wedding because you changed your name?" I asked.

"Not just that," she said.

I waited.

"I also admitted that I'm really Queens, not Manhattan. That my father is a plumber, not an investment banker. That my mother is a cashier at a diner, not a fund-raiser."

Ah.

"He said I'm a phony and a fake and the wedding's off," she said, breaking down again in sobs.

"Philippa, I'll bet that Parker just feels as blown away by the information as I do. You just need to explain why you felt you had to change your name and some details of your background. The important thing for him to know is how hard you've worked to lead yourself to him."

She stopped crying. "That's exactly what I did, isn't it? Parker is everything I've ever wanted."

"Go tell him," I said.

She brightened. "Will you hang out for a little while until I make myself look decent?" she asked.

I nodded. "You bet."

She hugged me. "I'm really glad you're my maid of honor, Eloise. Although, at my wedding, you'll be my *matron* of honor. You'll be a married woman by then."

"Philippa, do you ever get cold feet?" I asked her. "Or are you one hundred percent sure that Parker Gersh is the man for you?"

"Oh, I know he's the one," she said, applying her trademark pink lipstick.

"How?" I asked. "How are you so sure?"

"Because he feels like home."

"You're the third person who's said that in response to the question," I told her.

So why was I the only one who didn't understand what that meant? What did home feel like?

Incomplete. Like something is missing.

That was what my apartment felt like to me when Noah wasn't there, which was usually.

So if A plus B equaled C, then Noah felt like home.

Which, in my neighborhood, wasn't a good thing.

"Look at what Acid just dropped in my in-box," Philippa said the next day at work, waving a memo over the top rim of my cubicle. She let it flutter down; it landed on my keyboard.

Wow Weddings Memorandum

To: Philippa Wills
From: Astrid O'Connor
Re: *Wow Weddings*'s Today's Bride Feature: Classic Bride
Dear Philippa:
Please advise as to your premarital status. Yesterday you verbalized that you and your fiancé are no longer planning to marry. As such, *Wow Weddings* will need to find a new Classic Bride and reshoot at considerable expense. We will need to know, no later than start of the workday on Monday, if we must cancel your contract. —AO

Philippa spit on the memo and crumpled it into a ball and three-point shot it into my wastepaper basket. "Poor Philippa," she singsonged. "I, Queen Bee Acid O'Connor, am oh-so-sorry that you and Parker are having problems and that the wedding has been called off! Why don't you take the morning off and go talk to your fiancé? Don't you even give this silly feature a thought. After all, what's more important—the rest of your life or a magazine that no one reads anyway?"

I laughed. "The magazine, of course!"

She smiled, then her face began crumpling and she dropped into my guest chair. "It's been two days, and he still won't take my calls or return them. I've gone to his apartment and to the *Hot News* office. He won't see me."

Brainstorm!

"Philippa, I have an idea. Have you written your *Why I Said Yes!* column yet?"

She shook her head.

"Write it," I told her. "Now. Fast. And then messenger it over to *Hot News.*"

"But he knows why I said yes. Because I love him. Because I want to spend the rest of my life with him."

"But tell him *why,* Philippa. Tell him exactly why. Parker's a journalist. He'll respond to the written word."

"You think?" she asked, her entire expression brightening.

"I think. And hurry up. If it doesn't work, we'll need a new tactic. If you don't tell Acid the wedding's on by Monday, you're out of the feature."

"You know what? I really don't care about the stupid feature anymore," she said. "What am I getting? A wedding I don't want."

"A *free* wedding you don't want," I reminded her.

She shook her head. "I just want Parker." She bit her lip. "I guess it would be nice to have a big wedding with all the trimmings, even if it's not exactly the wedding I'd plan for myself. I don't want to go to City Hall. I've always dreamed of the whole thing—the gown, the flowers, the tables for ten."

I smiled. "Then you'd better get busy writing this all down for your *Why I Said Yes!* column."

She flew away from my cubicle and into her own. Moments later, I heard the fast clicking of her keyboard.

An hour later, I heard the fast clicking of Astrid O'Connor's and Mini-Astrid's heels in the hallway.

"Philippa!" Astrid barked. "What is this?"

I peered through the doorway of the cubicle. Astrid was standing in front of Philippa's cubicle, waving a few pieces of paper.

"What's what, Astrid?" Philippa asked, blue eyes innocent.

"Why don't I read this aloud," Astrid threatened, "and we'll see if you really want our tens of thousands of readers to know this…*information.*"

Philippa crossed her arms over her chest. "Go right ahead," she said.

"'*Why I Said Yes!* by Philippa Wills,'" Astrid began slowly in a singsong voice.

"So far, so good," Philippa said.

Astrid glared at her, then at the paper in her hand. "'I said yes to Parker Gersh because when I'm with him, I'm the most me,'" she read.

"Is that what you have a problem with?" Philippa asked her.

All eyes swung to Astrid.

"If I may continue without interruption," Astrid snapped. She cleared her throat. "'Let me start at the beginning,'" she read. "'I was born in Flushing, Queens—'" she raised her voice "'—to Brenda and Harold *Wilschitz*. They named me Phyllis.'" She raised her voice again. "*Phyllis Wilschitz.*" She glanced at Philippa. "Shall I continue?" Astrid asked, triumph in her voice.

"Oh, please do," Philippa responded.

"I think I've read quite enough," Astrid said. "My dear girl, I am all for self-improvement. If my parents had named me Agnes O'Dickwad, I would have changed it to Astrid O'Connor in a heartbeat."

Mini-Astrid burst out laughing, then clamped a hand over her mouth.

"However," Astrid continued, "your column, as is, does not reflect the mind-set of the Classic Bride."

"The Classic Bride wouldn't have changed the name her parents gave her?" I asked.

Astrid smiled at me. "Exactly."

I affected Philippa's innocent expression. "But doesn't tradition dictate that Today's Classic Bride *change* her name to her husband's?"

Astrid glared at me. A cool glare. An *I have never liked you or your stupid haircut* glare. Then she turned her attention to Philippa. "As *Wow Weddings's* Classic Bride, Philippa—or Phyllis, rather—you must write your column from the perspective of a traditional woman. Our advertisers are looking to you to be their voice, their model for all their products."

"My first name is *Philippa.* I am Philippa Wills. And that's who I'll be for the rest of my life. I'm not changing my last name when I marry Parker—if he'll still marry me, that is. And I'm not changing the column. Why I said yes is on those pages in your hand. It's the truth."

"That's all well and good, Philippa," Astrid said. "However, I wasn't aware that you had final approval of anything."

"Of myself, I do," Philippa replied. "Of my future, of my personal life, I do."

"Let me make myself very clear," Astrid said. "If you are not going to cooperate with the needs of the feature, with the needs of *Wow Weddings's* readership, you must resign. If you are not in my office by 9:00 a.m. sharp on Monday to let me know that the wedding is indeed on and that you will cooperate, I will null and void your contract. Do I make myself clear?"

"Crystal," Philippa said.

"And by the way, Philippa," Astrid added. "Despite your current engagement issues, I do expect you to be present for the reception-site selection shoot tomorrow and the registry-selection shoot on Friday. Per your contract with the magazine for the Today's Bride feature."

"I wouldn't miss either shoot for the world," Philippa said.

Astrid glared at Philippa, then rolled her eyes and clicked down the hall, Mini-Astrid following, her pen fly-

ing over her pad as Astrid barked notes for finding a po-
tential replacement for the Classic Bride.

I shook Philippa's hand. "Good job, kid."

She smiled. "Let's just hope Parker thinks so, too."

"This is where we're getting married?" Philippa asked
as we arrived at a nondescript—ugly, really—office building in midtown. The building was sandwiched between
a cell-phone store and a deli with a blinking neon OPEN
24 HOURS sign.

"*If* you're even getting married, Philippa," Astrid said,
whirling around to glare at her. "In any event, I'd appreciate it if you could hold your comments until you've seen
the space."

Yes, ma'am, Philippa mouthed at her back.

The *Wow Weddings* staff and our bridal parties squeezed
into a wood-paneled elevator. Astrid pressed the button
marked Penthouse.

"Be optimistic," Jane whispered to me. "You never
know."

I knew, all right. My expectations were very low.

A woman wearing crazy eyeglasses like Astrid's was
waiting for us as we exited the elevator. "Good afternoon!
I'm Vanessa Gumm, founder of Fifth Avenue Fantasy. I'm
so excited to show you the fantasy-wedding rooms we've
created for the Classic Bride and the Modern Bride! Let's
begin with the Modern Bride."

She led us down the hall to an ordinary-looking door.
An index card reading MB was taped onto it.

"Modern Bride, close your eyes," Vanessa said. "You're
about to step into your wedding-fantasy space!"

I closed my eyes and prayed.

The door opened.

My eyes opened.

My mouth opened.

The large room was four walls and a ceiling made entirely of metal panels. It looked like the inside of a paddy wagon. Dotted around the room were triangle-shaped tables and square metal seats without backs.

There wasn't a flower to be seen.

Instead, there were feathers. Feathers galore. In giant colored-glass vases on the tables. On the walls.

Mini-Astrid beamed.

Devlin snorted.

Philippa seemed enchanted.

Jane, Amanda, Natasha and Beth stared.

"I'll bet its termite free," Amanda joked.

"Too bad," I whispered, "because only termites would eat the food we're serving at the wedding."

"I love how the feather theme connects to the Modern Bride's gown," Mini-Astrid gushed.

As the *Wow Weddings* staff chitchatted and discussed minutiae changes with Vanessa (no one asked for my opinion, of course), and my friends glanced around with raised eyebrows, all I could think was that there were no windows.

What if I needed to make a sudden escape, say, a minute into the reading of the vows, when Noah promised to do anything till death did us part?

Could he really promise anything?

I suddenly felt claustrophobic.

"On to the Classic Bride's space," Astrid said, snapping her fingers.

Philippa glanced at me. "Heavy on the chintz, no doubt."

Vanessa led us down the hall to a door marked CB. "Classic Bride, close your eyes!"

Philippa and I both closed our eyes.

When I opened mine, Philippa's were still closed.

I nudged her in the ribs. "Philippa, it's okay. It's beautiful!"

It was. White gauze draped down from the ceiling, entwined with thousands of pastel roses. Round tables, covered with lacy tablecloths. Exquisite short vases with blooming roses. Candelabra.

Philippa's eyes popped open. She glanced around, grimacing. "It looks like my mother-in-law-to-be's living room," she whispered. "Nice, but *bor-ing.* Tell you what. I'll trade you. This grandma stuff is yours for fifty cents."

I laughed. *That* I could afford.

Ah, if only.

chapter 19

While china-pattern shopping in a tiny SoHo house-wares store with the *Wow* crowd and Grams, who smiled despite her reservations about formal dinnerware that was both gunmetal-colored and stamped with a silver, non-sensical Make Food Not War, I learned that Emmett had moved into Grams's spare bedroom.

"Charla's pregnant, isn't she?" Grams whispered as Devlin's assistant wiped off her coral lipstick and replaced it with dark red. Her quilted navy vest was exchanged for an orange leather jacket, borrowed from one of the saleswomen.

"*Grandmère,*" Devlin said, "please turn slightly to the left and hold the dish up just a fraction higher. Yes, that's it. No, look at the dish, not Eloise. Yes, hold that approving gaze...."

"How do you know?" I asked her.

Grams tried her best to freeze her smile onto her face. "Charla stopped by yesterday to ask if he was there. And before I even said yes, she went racing for the bathroom. I heard her trying to throw up as quietly as possible."

"She's been suffering from morning sickness a lot lately," I confirmed.

"She and Emmett talked for a bit in his room," Grams said. "And then she left, crying."

Oh no.

"Then Emmett left for a while, and I heard him come home very late," Grams said. "I've been wanting to talk to him about it, but I'm afraid I'll scare him into running away again."

"I'll talk to him tonight," I assured her. "Any tips?"

"This is your mother's grandbaby," Grams said. "That's all he needs to know."

My mouth dropped open. "Emmett and I have been so focused on our father and his legacy that neither of us has even thought about this baby being just as much Mom's as Theo Manfred's."

Grams nodded. "This baby will be more your mother's than your father's. You and Emmett are your *mother's* children. Not your father's. And this baby will be hers, too."

I grabbed Grams into a fierce hug.

"Now, that's perfect!" Devlin said, clicking away. "That's the money shot."

Over beer and buffalo wings at a bar near Grams's apartment, Emmett insisted he didn't break up with Charla.

"I'm just figuring things out," he said.

"Again."

"Yes, again," he snapped.

"And from here."

"Yeah, from here," he muttered.

"From a distance."

He shook his head and dipped a wing into hot sauce. "I don't need a lecture."

What do you need? I wondered. "Are you going to run forever, Emmett? If a baby with the woman you love won't keep you around, what will?"

"Who says I love Charla?" he snapped.

"I know you do."

But I didn't know. I thought so, but I wasn't sure. If he loved her, would he act like this?

Things aren't black and white, Eloise....

"Even if I do," he said. "Oh, forget it. You don't understand me, anyway."

"Emmett, can I tell you something?"

"You're *asking?* Someone call the *Daily News!* No, someone call *Ripley's Believe It Or Not!*"

"Hysterical," I said. "Emmett, I was talking to Grams this afternoon. She knows Charla's pregnant."

"You told her?" he bellowed. "I told you that *I* would tell when *I* was ready!"

"I didn't tell her. She figured it out yesterday."

"Oh," he said, taking a sip of beer.

"And she reminded me of something, Emmett. Something really important."

"What?" he asked.

"Are your ears open? Really open?"

"Jesus, Eloise, just tell me."

Please let this work... "I know you're scared out of your mind about this baby. I know you're worried that you don't know how to do this, how to be committed to someone, how to be a husband or a father or how to risk what staying put means."

"Oh, God, here we go again. My sister, the shrink."

"Emmett, just listen, okay?"

He bit into a wing and stared straight ahead.

"I think you should remember that you're Mom's son. You're her child. First and foremost. And this baby, your baby, is Mom's grandchild. Hers."

He glanced at me. "And?"

"And I think you're focusing too much on who your father is instead of who your mother was."

The moment the words were out of my mouth, I realized how guilty I was of that very thing.

He was silent for a moment.

"I feel like I'm going to throw up," he said. "I think I have sympathy morning sickness."

I was surprised. "You know about sympathy morning sickness?"

"Charla gave me a book for first-time fathers."

I smiled and squeezed his hand. "If you feel sick, Emmett, it's because this is life-changing stuff you're dealing with. It's understandable."

"Well, maybe I don't want to deal with it," he said. "Maybe I just want something else."

"Like what?" I asked.

"Like my freedom. I'm only twenty-nine years old. Maybe I want to travel or write a screenplay or join the army. Maybe I want to see Tibet."

"Tibet's your best bet," I said. "I doubt monks have cell phones or Internet access. You'd be really unreachable in a monastery, Emmett. Is that what you want to be for this baby—unreachable?"

You can't do to this kid what our father did to us. What Charla's did to her. You can't.

"I don't need this crap," he said and walked out.

In the immortal words of Yogi Berra, it was déjà vu all over again.

★ ★ ★

On Saturday morning, I left a message for Emmett with my grandmother that Charla and I were leaving for Pennsylvania at 9:00 a.m. sharp.

He pounded on my door at a minute to nine. "Why is Charla coming? What does she have to do with this?"

"Theo Manfred is her baby's biological grandfather," I said. "That's what she has to do with it."

"And Eloise is my baby's aunt," Charla added. "I'm supporting her. I've been down the road she's going."

"Shit," he muttered.

I cupped my hand around my ear. "What was that, Emmett? I don't think the baby heard you."

"I really don't need this crap," he said.

"Yes, you do," Charla said as we walked around the corner to the car-rental agency.

Glummer than ever, Emmett got in the car, another Chevy. "I'm only going with you so that when we find him, I can punch him out."

I put the key in the ignition. "So you've said."

"Wendy," Charla said, putting on her seat belt.

"What?" I asked her.

"Wendy. Girls' names that start with W."

"Winona," I said.

"Wanda," Emmett muttered, and we were on our way.

A hundred wrong turns and two nonexistent addresses later, including the Scranton newspaper that had gone out of business six years ago, we arrived at a gas station where Theo Manfred had pumped gas and painted landscapes—as of five months ago.

It was the closest we'd come to him.

"That's his easel," the manager said. "He just up and quit

one day. Never came back, but he left the easel. Guess he felt guilty for not giving me notice. I'm not much of a painter, though."

"Do you happen to have his last known address?" Charla asked.

"I should," the man replied. "Let me check my Rolodex."

"That's okay," Emmett said. "We don't need it."

Charla touched his arm. "Emmett, we've come all this way...."

He released his seat belt. "Fine, you guys go. I'll hitch a ride home."

"Emmett," Charla said. "What are you so afraid of?"

"I'm not *afraid* of anything. I just don't see the point of finding him. What are we going to do when we meet him—make small talk? Ask him how he's been for the last twenty-seven years?"

"The point is to make some kind of peace with something that happened to you," Charla said.

Emmett rolled his eyes. "I just want to get the hell away from here. I want to go home." But he didn't get out of the car. He burst into tears and covered his face with his hands. And then he put his hands around Charla's face. "I love you. I really do."

"I know, Emmett," she said, pulling him to her. "I've always known that."

"I'm sorry I've been such a loser," he said. He put his hand on her belly. "I won't let you down again."

Now it was Charla's and my turn to start bawling.

The gas station manager rapped on my window. I rolled it down. "Do you want the address or not?"

I glanced at Emmett.

He nodded.

★ ★ ★

Four minutes later, we were there. 452 Lummox Road was the last house on the right of a dead-end street with no sidewalks. The house, like the ones beside it, was ramshackle, in need of paint and a handyman. There was a mailbox out front with two names spelled with black stickers. Green and Manfred.

I put the car in park and turned off the ignition, but neither I nor Emmett moved a muscle. For a half hour.

A woman came out of the front door wearing a puffy down coat like Charla's. She was fiftyish and pretty, with sandy-blond hair. She stood on the step for a moment eyeing the car, then came over.

She rapped on Emmett's window, and he looked at me, then lowered it. "If you're casing the place, I'll tell you right now, the most valuable thing I own is a nineteen-inch TV set and a bottle of red wine that I won at a Christmas-party raffle. So if you're gonna come take it, come. But stop freaking me out by sitting out here."

"We're not burglars," Charla assured her.

"Does a Theo Manfred live here?" I asked her, gesturing at the mailbox.

"Past tense, hon," the woman said. "He lived here with me for seven months, then split a little over a month ago for Florida to go into some stupid shrimp business with a buddy."

I glanced past her at the house where my father had lived, slept, eaten, breathed, drunk beer or done whatever he did, as of a month ago. I tried to connect him to me and couldn't. The man who'd lived here, whose name was still on the mailbox, whose name my brother and I—and his and Charla's baby—had, wasn't my father; he was just a man who'd had a relationship with my mother, biologically helped produce two children, and then decided that particular life with those particular people weren't making him happy. And so he left.

That wasn't a father.

His leaving had nothing to do with me and nothing to do with Emmett and, I was sure, nothing to do with my mother. It had everything to do with Theo Manfred and whoever he was. And whoever he was, he'd missed out on a lot. He'd gotten exactly what he deserved.

"How do you all know him?" the woman asked. "Work?"

I shook my head. "We met him when he was traveling."

She nodded. "Yup, he's sure good at that."

"Well, if you're headed South, you'll find him in—" She stopped, tapping her finger against her forehead. "Huh. I can never remember the name of the town. It's on the tip of my tongue," she said. "If you give me a minute, I'll think of it."

Emmett and I looked at each other.

"That's okay," I said. "We don't need to know."

"You're sure?" Emmett asked me.

I nodded. "Dead sure."

"Suit yourselves," the woman said, and headed back inside the house.

I turned the car around and drove about a quarter mile or so, then pulled over near the highway. My legs were shaking.

I glanced in the rearview mirror at Emmett. "We don't need to actually find *him*," I said. "I never realized that."

Emmett nodded. "I think the answers were in the looking, if that makes any sense."

I turned around and reached out my hand to him. After a few seconds, he took my hand and held it.

★ ★ ★

New York City, 14 miles. I peered at Emmett and Charla in the rearview mirror. She was asleep. Emmett was looking out the window, his hand on her belly.

I came home to an empty apartment, but evidence of Noah was everywhere. Not just tangible evidence, either. He was with me. He was home.

If you need me, just call.

I picked up the phone and dialed his cell phone. Noah picked up immediately. "Is everything okay? Is something wrong? Did you find him?"

"Everything's okay," I said. "We didn't find him. We decided we found what we needed along the way."

"I'm coming home tonight," he said. "I'll make you my best lasagna."

"Can't wait."

chapter 20

On Monday morning at 8:59, Philippa burst into Astrid's office and announced that the wedding was on.

The entire office clapped.

Philippa's fake family was pretending to be skipping along a path in Central Park. The models stood in front of the summer-day backdrop, kicking up their feet and throwing back their heads in delight.

"Can you try to cry a few tears of joy, Mom?" Devlin said to the fake Mrs. Wills. "And, Dad, a little more pride in your expression." Fake Mr. Wills puffed out his chest and gazed at Philippa as though she'd just won the Miss America pageant.

Philippa held up her hands. Devlin put down his camera. "Classic Bride, can you get your hands out of the frame?"

"I can't do it," Philippa said.

"You can't do what, Philippa?" Astrid asked, examining her nails.

"I can't do this, any of it! I won't have a fake family!"

"What is she talking about?" Astrid said, throwing up her own hands. "Will someone tell me what she's talking about?"

"I hired fakes," Philippa shouted. "They're not my family. They're just stand-ins!"

Astrid waved Devlin back over. "Philippa, I don't care *who's* in the photos as long as they look remotely like you and have a Classic appeal."

"Well, I do care who's in the photos!" Philippa yelped.

The studio door opened and three people came inside, a fiftyish couple and a twenty-something guy who also looked a lot like Philippa.

"Phyl? Are we too late?" asked a woman with a heavy Queens accent.

Philippa whirled around. "Are you here? You're really here? And what happened to you guys? You all look so...so..."

"Like you?" her brother asked. "We spent a little time with the personal shoppers in Bloomingdale's."

"You did all this for me? But I thought you hated me."

Mrs. Wilschitz's eyes filled with tears. "Phyllie, we don't hate you. How could you think such a thing? We love you. So much."

"But I thought—" Philippa began.

"No," her father interrupted. "We thought we were so wronged, and then we found out what wronged really meant."

"Do you remember Gertie and Bill Ross down the hall in 4A?" Mrs. Wilschitz asked. "You used to baby-sit their Annie—the one with all the gorgeous curly hair. Well,

Gertie and Bill just found out that Annie has cancer. Cancer, at nineteen. That's being *wronged*."

Mr. Wilschitz nodded. "Phyllie, we love you. We just want you to be happy. And if Philippa Wills is who you are, then that's who you are."

"We accept you for who you are or aren't," her mother added. "We don't care what your name is. We're just glad you're healthy and happy."

Philippa broke down in tears amid a chorus of aw's from the *Wow*ers. There were hugs and kisses all around.

Astrid looked confused, then bored, then snapped and said, "Places, people."

"Eloise, where is your family or your stand-ins?" Astrid asked, glancing around the studio.

"My family is right there," I said, pointing to the bagel buffet.

She eyed the group mingling around the cream cheese. Noah, Grams, Dottie and Herbert Benjamin, Emmett, Charla, Jane, Amanda, Natasha, baby Summer and even Beth Benjamin stood splitting open bagels and sipping coffee and orange juice. There was a debate over fresh versus pulpy juice. Whether everything bagels were too much. If fat-free cream cheese tasted like cardboard. If Amanda's best side was her right or left. If Jane should smile open- or close-mouthed. If Natasha should change her stance and allow Summer to be the child-model-slash-actress Devlin thought she should be.

This was my family. Last night, Noah called his parents and sister; I called my friends and Emmett and Grams, and when I arrived at work this morning, they were all waiting in the reception area with Kevin Costnerly.

Oops. I sent him on his way at a loss of two hundred

fifty bucks. I'd never been so happy to throw away money in my life.

"Eloise," Astrid said, "I see your bridal party, your in-laws-to-be and your fiancé. I do not see your father or a stand-in. We're shooting your father-daughter shots today along with the family shots."

"I don't have a father," I told Astrid.

"Everyone has a father," she replied with her accompanying eyeroll.

I shook my head. "Not me. My father left my mother, brother and me when I was five. We haven't seen or heard from him since. I don't have a father."

Mouths stopped chewing and talking. Everyone's eyes were on me. For once, I didn't care.

Astrid smiled tightly. "Well you *have* a father, he's just not in your life. Dear, I would think you would know that at a magazine, semantics are everything."

Ignore her. Ignore her. Ignore her.

"My point is," I said, "that I don't have a father and therefore, there won't be a father in my family-photo shots."

She handed me a Rolodex card. "Just call Perfect People. Say you're looking for a Billy Bob Thornton type with a full head of hair."

"Astrid, I don't want to pretend I have a father. I don't *need* to pretend. Especially not for something that involves my future, my wedding."

She held up a hand, her palm almost in my face. "What am I thinking?" she said, which was rhetorical for I'm-having-a-brainstorm-everyone-shut-up. "What am I thinking?"

We all stared at her.

"The Modern Bride's father *shouldn't* walk her down

the aisle—that is so traditional!" She smiled and pointed one of her beige claws at me. "Eloise, call your dad and tell him we won't be needing him for your family shots unless you absolutely want him in the pictures. I'd prefer that your brother—or better yet, a gay female friend— walk you down the aisle in the ceremony and in the shots we'll take of a 'practice walk.'"

My nearest and dearest were all staring at Astrid as though she had four heads.

I smiled at Astrid. "Okay, boss, whatever you say. I'll call my dad right now and let him know I won't be needing him after all."

"Great," she praised. "Eloise, I must say, you've been most cooperative throughout this entire process. I'm very pleased."

I would get her. I wasn't sure exactly what I would do to Acid O'Connor, but I would get her somehow. Hide anchovies in her desk? Cancel her home telephone?

No.

I knew exactly what I was going to do. And I needed my partner in crime.

Make that my partners in crime.

The Flirt Night Round Table added three more seats to its weekly meetings. At an Upper West Side coffee lounge, Jane, Amanda, Natasha, baby Summer, Philippa, Charla, Beth Benjamin and I sat around a scarred wooden coffee table full of coffee drinks and goodies. I couldn't wait to share my master plan for the ultimate annoying of Astrid O'Connor.

"See," Charla said, sipping her hot mocha. "Isn't soy milk absolutely delicious in coffee?"

Philippa sipped her latte. "I, for one, love it!"

The moment we arrived, Philippa had taken a note-book out of her tote bag and announced she'd be happy to take minutes. I tried to tell her our get-togethers weren't that formal, but she wanted to remember her first official hang-out with girlfriends.

Beth Benjamin brought her divorce decree and actu-ally got up on the table and did a little jig before one of the post-teens behind the counter rushed over to tell her she couldn't do that.

"Sorry," Beth said to us as she hopped down. "I know you're all either getting married or are happily married, but I've never been so happy to be officially single in my entire life!"

We clapped.

"Eloise," Beth added, "I'll wear whatever you want me to wear at your wedding, because you know what?"

"What?"

"It's not about the stupid dress," she said. "It's about the guy. I had the wrong one, that's all."

"Amen," I said.

And we all clinked our coffees.

"But you know what, Beth? You're not going to wear that rubber dress, after all. None of you are."

"We're not?" Jane asked.

"Nope. *Another* lucky bridal party will be modeling the rubber look on leap year. You'll all be wearing a floaty pink satin number instead. A dress that would do Audrey Hepburn proud."

Understanding dawned on Philippa's face. "Yay!" she shouted.

"Yay," baby Summer repeated, clapping her hands.

chapter 21

"I have only two and a half minutes," Astrid said to me and Philippa as we were ushered into her office. "I have a meeting with the caterers at five." As she gestured at the twin toile-covered guest chairs in front of her huge mahogany desk, I had a vision of Philippa and me jumping up and down and shouting our yeses in response to her offer of the free dream weddings.

"Astrid," I began, "Philippa and I are both very appreciative of our free dream weddings. However, we've come to a rather startling conclusion about ourselves."

"Very startling," Philippa added.

Astrid narrowed her eyes at us.

"It turns out that, despite my haircut and weird shoes and arty job, *I'm* the Classic Bride," I said.

"And I, despite my headband and penny loafers, am the Modern Bride," Philippa said.

"I don't have time for this," Astrid responded with an

eyeroll. She picked up a stack of memos on her desk. "*Wow Weddings* doesn't have time for this."

"We'll be succinct, then," I said. "We want to switch weddings."

Astrid let out a dry laugh. "Even if I would allow such a thing, it's impossible. We've shot the entire feature. We have dresses on order. We would have to gather your bridal parties, your fiancés, your families and reshoot the various selections. We've already had to reshoot your sibling photos, Philippa. We'd have to re-size, re-alter—"

"That sounds right to me," I said. "Resizing."

Astrid rolled her eyes. "My dear girls, your passionate youth is endearing. Really, however—"

"Either we switch or we walk," Philippa said.

Astrid glared at her. "Excuse me?"

"We want to switch weddings," I said again. I could explain; I could tell her why and what and how and where, but we'd be wasting our breath.

Instead, we let the words hang in the air.

We stared at her. She stared at us.

"We reshoot and resize at your expense," Astrid finally said. "And instead of a two-week honeymoon, you'll only get one week. The other week you'll spend working to help make up lost time and expense."

"That'll be just fine," Philippa said. "A honeymoon is traditionally two weeks, so it's better that mine will be only one."

"Especially since you'll be in Chicago in late February," I added.

Astrid rolled her eyes and buzzed her assistant.

"Surprise!"

I glanced up from my desk. A diamond ring, a very nice diamond ring, was twinkling over the rim of my cubicle.

"I know that finger!" I said, racing around the cubicle. Though I'd know Charla's sparkly purple nail polish anywhere, it was the ring I knew.

My grandmother's marquis diamond with the sapphire baguettes.

Charla, her blond pigtails swinging against her shoulders as she twirled around and wiggled the fingers on her left hand, was beaming. Emmett, aw-shucks expression on his face, stood next to her, his hands stuffed into his pockets.

"You won't consider it stealing your thunder if we get married first, will you?" Charla asked me.

"Please steal it," I said, wrapping them in a hug. "Congratulations. And welcome to the family, Charla. I'm so happy for you both."

"We want to do it tomorrow at City Hall," Emmett said. "You, Grams and Charla's mom. She's flying in from Oregon tonight."

I couldn't think of a more perfect way to get married.

Blank page. Blinking cursor.

Why I Said Yes! by Eloise Manfred, *Wow Weddings*'s Classic Bride.

I said yes because Noah Benjamin feels like home. The end.

epilogue

I have attended three weddings in as many weeks. First, Charla and Emmett's at City Hall (which in Manhattan was really just the city clerk's office in all its scuffed-lino-leum-lack-of-grandeur-and-romance). But Charla and Emmett dressed to the nines; she in a stunning white sleeveless gown with elbow-length gloves (her honey-colored pigtails transformed into an elegant chignon at the nape of her neck), and Emmett, more handsome than I'd ever seen him, in a black tux. Grams, Charla's mom, and Noah and I stood sniffling as Emmett gently dipped his bride in a whopper of a kiss. Afterward, we went to a popular supper club for dinner and dancing, and tourists took pictures of the bride and groom.

Wedding number two was Philippa's. Philippa and I split the cost of reordering and reshooting and just about everything else connected to our free dream weddings, but it was worth it. Dottie Benjamin and her husband were so thrilled that Beth wouldn't have to wear a Halloween costume to her brother's wedding that they contributed a thousand dollars to the cause as a wedding gift. Philippa's and my bridal party and fiancés and families had had to gather together at the last minute for an entire week of reshooting, but everyone had shown up with smiles.

And so on Leap Year Day, February 29, a spectacularly sunny, clear and cold winter evening, Philippa Wills married Parker Gersh in the bizarro room of Fifth Avenue Fantasies. Parker's preppy sisters looked confused in their rubber dresses. One tried to slip on a pearl necklace, but Astrid put an end to that.

Parker proudly showed everyone his square rust wedding band. And Mrs. Willschitz, who only slipped once with a *Phylli*— but caught herself and changed the emphasis of the syllable at the last second—was a trouper in her dark yellow perforated-leather mother-of-the-Modern-Bride ensemble.

With her friends, family and many strangers surrounding her, Philippa danced the night away in her Big Bird gown, her peace veil flopping, her yellow feathers ruffling. A drunken uncle requested the chicken dance, but no one got the joke.

Today was wedding number three: mine. The first day of spring was a warm and sunny sixty-two degrees. Very early in the morning, Emmett and I met at St. Monica's Church to light a candle for our mom. As I sat in my usual pew, my brother most unusually sitting next to me, I wasn't thinking of losses. Only of gains. My mother's dream for me was to marry, to not let other people dictate my happiness, my future, and today, I was making my mother proud.

In the CB room of Fifth Avenue Fantasy, a few family

members, a few friends, way too many co-workers and countless strangers in witness, Emmett walked me down the aisle, a pink and white carpet strewn with pink and white rose petals. When he lifted my veil, white tulle, not yellow leather, there were tears in his eyes.

"I'm not really giving you *away*," Emmett said as he led me to Noah.

I hugged him like crazy.

Jane, Amanda, Natasha, Philippa, Beth, baby Summer and Charla, who I insisted be a bridesmaid (Acid had relented after I threatened to wear my tiny green dinosaur earrings for the photo montage that would appear in July's issue), looked beautiful in their *Midsummer Night's Dream* Audrey Hepburn dresses. My grandmother, in ivory sequins, sobbed during the entire ceremony.

Noah and I couldn't wait to run around Walt Disney World, shaking hands with Mickey and riding child-size trains through Daffy Duck tunnels. We could use a little eighty-degree weather, our plain gold wedding bands gleaming in the warm sun, shiny and new like us, like our marriage, like me.

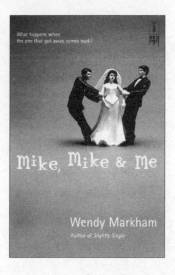

New from Cathy Yardley,
author of *L.A. Woman*

Couch World

Welcome to COUCH WORLD where life is simple
for the *über*hip P.J., who wakes up at 2:00 p.m.
in someone else's place on someone else's
couch. Showers. Clothes. And goes to work as
a punter—someone who fills in for a DJ who
is unable to make a gig. But life for P.J. gets
complicated when a reporter infiltrates her life
and acts as if P.J.'s life is her own.

**Available wherever
trade paperbacks
are sold.**

RED DRESS INK
™

Also available from Melissa Senate

See Jane Date

Melissa Senate has captured the essence of being single in NYC, wryly portraying all the fun and the annoyances that come with the title!

RED DRESS INK ™

The Solomon Sisters Wise Up

by Melissa Senate

Meet the Solomon sisters:

Sarah—six weeks pregnant by a guy she's dated for two months.

Ally—recently discovered her "perfect" husband cheating on her.

Zoe—a dating critic who needs to listen to her own advice.

Suddenly finding themselves sharing a bedroom in Daddy's Park Avenue Penthouse, the Solomon sisters are about to wise up, and find allies in each other, in this heartwarming and hilarious novel by Melissa Senate, author of *See Jane Date*.

RDI12031-TRR

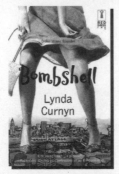